# The Builders

# Also by Daniel Polansky

# THE BUILDERS

## DANIEL POLANSKY

A TOM DOHERTY ASSOCIATES BOOK

NEW YORK

THE BUILDERS

Edited by Justin Landon

A Tor.com Book

Published by Tom Doherty Associates, LLC

175 Fifth Avenue

New York, NY 10010


www.tor.com


Tor® is a registered trademark of Tom Doherty Associates, LLC.


ISBN 978-0-7653-8400-3 (e-book)

ISBN 978-0-7653-8530-7 (trade paperback)


First Edition: November 2015

*To my uncles Theodore, Frank, and John,*
*for long years of love and support*

# PART THE FIRST

# Chapter 1

# A Mouse Walks into a Bar . . .

Reconquista was cleaning the counter with his good hand when the double doors swung open. He squinted his eye at the light, the stub of his tail curling around his peg leg. "We're closed."

Its shadow loomed impossibly large from the threshold, tumbling over the loose warped wood of the floorboards, swallowing battered tables and splintered chairs within its inky bulk.

"You hear me? I said we're closed," Reconquista repeated, this time with a quiver that couldn't be mistaken for anything else.

The outline pulled its hat off and blew a fine layer of grime off the felt. Then it set it back on its head and stepped inside.

Reconquista's expression shifted, fear of the unknown replaced with fear of the known-quite-well. "Captain . . . I . . . I didn't recognize you."

Penumbra shrunk to the genuine article, it seemed

absurd to think the newcomer had inspired such terror. The Captain was big for a mouse, but then being big for a mouse is more or less a contradiction in terms, so there's not much to take there. The bottom of his trench coat trailed against the laces of his boots, and the broad brim of his hat swallowed the narrow angles of his face. Absurd indeed. Almost laughable.

Almost—but not quite. Maybe it was the ragged scar that ran from his forehead through the blinded pulp of his right eye. Maybe it was the grim scowl on his lips, a scowl that didn't shift a hair as the Captain moved deeper into the tavern. The Captain was a mouse, sure as stone; from his silvery-white fur to his bright pink nose, from the fan-ears folded back against his head to the tiny paws held tight against his sides. But rodent or raptor, mouse or wolf, the Captain was not a creature to laugh at.

He paused in front of Reconquista. For a moment he had the impression that the ice that held the Captain's features in place was about to melt, or at least unsettle. But it was a false impression. The faintest suggestion of greeting offered, the mouse walked to a table in the back and dropped himself lightly into one of the seats.

Reconquista had been a rat, once. The left side of his body still was, a firm if aging specimen of *Rattus norvegicus*. But the right half was an ungainly assortment of leather, wood, and cast iron, a jury-rigged contraption mimicking his lost flesh. In general it did a poor job, but then he wasn't full up with competing options.

"I'm the first?" the Captain asked in a high soprano, though none would have called it that to his face.

"*Si, si,*" said Reconquista, stutter-stepping on his peg leg out from behind the bar. On the hook attached to the stump of his right arm was slung an earthenware jug, labeled with an ominous trio of *x*'s. He set it down in front of the Captain with a thud. "You're the first."

The Captain popped the cork and tilted the liquor down his throat.

"Will the rest come?" Reconquista asked.

A half-second passed while the Captain filled his stomach with liquid fire. Then he set the growler back on the table and wiped his snout. "They'll be here."

Reconquista nodded and headed back to the bar to make ready. The Captain was never wrong. More would be coming.

# Chapter 2

# A Stoat and a Frenchman

Bonsoir was a stoat, that's the first thing that needs to be said. There are many animals that are like stoats, similar enough in purpose and design as to confuse the amateur naturalist—weasels, for instance, and ferrets. But Bonsoir was a stoat, and as far as he was concerned a stoat was as distinct from its cousins as the sun is from the moon. To mistake him for a weasel or, heaven forbid, a polecat—well, let's just say creatures who voiced that misimpression tended not to do so ever again. Creatures who voiced that misimpression tended, generally speaking, not to do anything ever again.

Now a stoat is a cruel animal, perhaps the cruelest in the Gardens. They are brought up to be cruel, they must be cruel—for nature, which is crueler, has dictated that their prey be children and the unborn, the beloved and the weak. And to that end nature has given them paws stealthy and swift, wide eyes to see clearly on a moonless night, and a soul utterly remorseless, without conscience or scruple. But that is nature's fault, and not the stoat's; the stoat is what it has been made to be, as are we all.

So Bonsoir was a stoat, but Bonsoir was not only a stoat. He was not even, perhaps, primarily a stoat. Bonsoir was also a Frenchman.

A Frenchman, as any Frenchman will tell you, is a difficult condition to abide, as much a privilege as a responsibility. To maintain the appropriate standards of excellence, this *superlative* of grace, was a burden not so light even in the homeland, and immeasurably more difficult in the colonies. Being both French and a stoat had resulted in a more or less constant crisis of self-identity—one which Bonsoir often worked to resolve, in classic Gallic fashion, via monologue.

And indeed, when the Captain had seen him some six weeks previous, Bonsoir was in the midst of expounding on his favorite subject to a captive audience. He had one hand draped around a big-bottomed squirrel resting on his knee, and with the other he pawed absently at the cards lying facedown on the table in front of him. "Sometimes, creatures in their ignorance have called me an ermine." His pointed nose trailed back and forth, the rest of his head following in train. "Do I look like an albino to you?"

There were five seats at the poker table but only three were filled, the height of Bonsoir's chip stack making clear what had reduced the count. The two remaining players, a pair of bleak, hard-looking rats, seemed less than enthralled by Bonsoir's lecture. They shifted aimlessly in their seats and shot each other angry looks, and they checked and rechecked their cards, as if hoping to find something different. They might have been brothers, or sisters, or friends, or hated enemies. Rats tend to look alike, so it's tough to tell.

"Now a stoat," Bonsoir continued, whispering the words into the ear of his mistress, "a stoat is black, black all over, black down to the tip of his"—he goosed the squirrel and she gave a little chuckle—"feet."

The Swollen Waters was a dive bar, ugly even for the ugly section of an ugly town, but busy enough despite this, or perhaps because of it. The pack of thugs, misanthropes, and hooligans who thronged the place took a good hard look at the Captain as he entered, searching for signs of easy prey. Seeing none, they fell back into their cups.

A swift summer storm had matted down the Captain's fur, and to reach a seat at the bar required an ungainly half-leap. He seemed more than usually perturbed, and he was usually quite perturbed.

"You want anything?" The server was a shrewish sort of shrew, as shrews tend to be.

"Whiskey."

A miserly dram poured into a stained glass. "We don't get many mice in here."

"We're not partial to the stench of piss," the captain said curtly.

Back at the table the river card had been laid, and Bonsoir's lady-friend rested on the vacant seat next to him. One rat was already out, the stack of chips too much weight for his wallet to support. But the other had stayed in, calling Bonsoir's raise with the remainder of his dwindling finances. Now he triumphantly tossed his cards down on the table and reached for the pot.

"That is a very fine hand," Bonsoir said, and somehow when he had finished this statement his paw was settled atop the rat's, firmly keeping him from withdrawing his winnings. "That is the sort of hand a fellow might expect to get rich from." Bonsoir flipped his own over, revealing a pair of minor nobles. "Such a fellow would be disappointed."

The rat looked hard at the two thin pieces of paper that had just lost him his savings. Then he looked back up at the stoat. "You've been taking an awful lot of pots tonight." His partner slid back from the table and rested his hand on a cap-and-ball pistol in his belt. "An awful lot of pots."

Bonsoir's eyes were cheery and vicious. "That is because you are a very bad poker player," he said, a toothy smile spreading across his snout, "and because I am Bonsoir."

The second rat tapped the butt of his weapon with a curved yellow nail, *tic tic,* reminding his partner of the play. Around them the other customers did what they could to prepare for the coming violence. Some shifted to the corners. Those within range of an exit chose this opportunity to slip out of it. The bartender ducked beneath the counter and considered sadly how long it would take to get the bloodstains out of his floor.

But after a moment the first rat blinked slowly, then shook his head at the second.

"That is what I like about your country," Bonsoir said, merging his new winnings with his old. "Everyone is so reasonable."

The story was that Bonsoir had come over with the Foreign Legion and never left. There were lots of stories about Bonsoir. Some of them were probably even true.

The rats at least seemed to think so. They slunk out the front entrance faster than dignity would technically allow—but then rats, as befits a species subsisting on filth, make no fetish of decorum.

The Captain let himself down from his high chair and made his way to the back table, now occupied solely by Bonsoir and his female companion. She had resumed her privileged position on his lap, and chuckled gaily at the soft things he whispered into her ear.

"*Cap-i-ton,*" Bonsoir offered by way of greeting, though he had noted the mouse when first he entered. "It has been a long time."

The Captain nodded.

"This is a social call? You have tracked down your old friend Bonsoir to see how he has accommodated to his new life?"

The Captain shook his head.

"No?" The stoat set his paramour aside a second time and feigned wide-eyed surprise. "I am shocked. Do you mean to say you have some ulterior motive in coming to see Bonsoir?"

"We're taking another run at it."

"We are taking another run at it?" Bonsoir repeated, scratching at his chin with one ebony claw. "Who is *we*?"

"The gang."

"Those who are still alive, you mean?"

The Captain didn't answer.

"And why do you think I would want to rejoin the . . . gang, as you say?"

"There'll be money on the back end."

Bonsoir waived his hand over the stack of chips in front of him. "There is always money."

"And some action. I imagine things get dull for you, out here in the sticks."

Bonsoir shivered with annoyance. So far as Bonsoir was concerned, the spot he occupied was the center of the world. "Do I look like Elf to you, so desperate to kill? Besides—there are always creatures willing to test Bonsoir."

"And of such caliber."

Bonsoir's upper lip curled back to reveal the white of a canine. "I am not sure I understand your meaning, my *Cap-i-ton.*"

"No?" The Captain pulled a cigar out of his pocket. It was short, thick, and stinky. He lit a match against the rough wood of the chair in front of him and held it to the end. "I think you've grown as fat as your playmate. I think wine and females have ruined you. I think you're happy here, intimidating the locals and playing lord. I think this was a waste of my time."

The Captain was halfway to the door when he felt the press of metal against his throat. "I am Bonsoir," the stoat hissed, a scant inch from the Captain's ears. "I have cracked rattlesnake eggs while their mother slept soundly atop them, I have snatched the woodpecker mid-flight. More have met their end at my hand than from corn liquor and poisoned bait! I am Bonsoir, whose steps fall without sound, whose knives are always sharp, who comes at night and leaves widows weeping in the morning."

The Captain showed no signs of excitement at his predicament, or surprise at the speed and quiet with which Bonsoir had managed to cross the distance between them. Instead he puffed out a dank blend of cigar smoke and continued casually, "So you're in?"

Bonsoir scooted round in front of the Captain, his temper again rising to the surface. "Do you think this is enough for Bonsoir? This shithole of a bar, these fools who let me take their money? Do you think Bonsoir would turn his back on the *Cap-i-ton*, on his comrades, on the cause?" The stoat grew furious at the suggestion, working himself into a chittering frenzy. "Bonsoir's hand is the *Cap-i-ton*'s! Bonsoir's heart is the *Cap-i-ton*'s! Let any creature who thinks otherwise say so now, that Bonsoir may satisfy the stain on his honor!"

Bonsoir twirled the knife in his palm and looked around to see if anyone would take up the challenge. None did. After a moment the Captain leaned in close and whispered, "St. Martin's Day. At the Partisan's bar."

Bonsoir's knife disappeared somewhere about his person. He chopped off a crisp salute, the first he had offered anyone in half a decade. "Bonsoir will be there."

# Chapter 3

# Bonsoir's Arrival

Bonsoir made a loud entrance for a quiet creature. The Captain had been sitting silently for half an hour when the double doors flew open and the stoat came sauntering in. It was too fast to be called saunter, really, Bonsoir bobbing and weaving to his own internal sense of rhythm—but it conveyed the same intent. A beret sat jauntily on his scalp, and a long black cigarette dangled from his lips. Strung over his shoulder was a faded green canvas sack. He carried no visible weapons, though somehow this did not detract from his sense of menace.

He nodded brusquely to Reconquista and slipped his way to the back, stopping in front of the main table. "Where is everyone?"

"They're coming."

Bonsoir took his beret off his head and scowled, then replaced it. "It is not right for Bonsoir to be the first—he is too special. His arrival deserves an audience."

The Captain nodded sympathetically, or as close as

he was able to with a face formed of granite. He passed Bonsoir the now half-empty jug as the stoat bounced against a stool. "They're coming," he repeated.

# Chapter 4

# The Virtues of Silence

Boudica lay half-buried in the creek bed when she noticed a figure threading its way along the dusty path leading up from town. The stream had been dry for years now, but the shifting silt at the bottom was still the coolest spot for miles, shaded as it was by the branches of a scrub tree. Most days, and all the hot ones, you could find Boudica there, whiling away the hours in mild contemplation, a hunk of chaw to keep her company.

When the figure was half a mile out, Boudica's eyebrows elevated a tick above their resting position. For the opossum, it was an extraordinary expression of shock. Indeed, it verged on hysteria. She reflected for a moment longer, than resettled her bulk into the sand.

This would mean trouble, and generally speaking, Boudica did not like trouble. Boudica, in fact, liked the absolute opposite of trouble. She liked peace and quiet, solitude and silence. Boudica lived for those occasional moments of perfect tranquility, when all noise and motion faded away to nothing, and time itself seemed to still.

That she sometimes broke that silence with the retort of a rifle was, in her mind, ancillary to the main issue. And indeed, it was not her steady hands that had made Boudica the greatest sniper who had ever sighted down a target. Nor her eyes, eyes that had picked out the Captain long moments before anyone else could have even identified him as a mouse. It was that she understood how to wait, to empty herself of everything in anticipation of that one perfect moment—and then to fill that moment with death.

As an expert, then, Boudica had no trouble biding the time it took the mouse to arrive, which she spent wondering how the Captain had found her. Not her spot at the creek bed; the locals were a friendly bunch and would have seen no harm in passing on that information. But the town itself was south of the old boundaries, indeed as south as one could go, surrounded by an impenetrably barren wasteland.

Boudica spat tobacco juice into the weeds and set her curiosity aside. The Captain was the sort of animal who accomplished the things he set out to do.

Finally the mouse crested the little hill that led up to Boudica's perch. The Captain reacted to the sight of his old comrade with the same lack of excitement that the opossum had displayed upon picking him out some twenty minutes prior. Though the heat was scorching, and the walk from town rugged, and the Captain no longer a pinky, he remained unwinded. As if to fix this, he reached into his duster and pulled out a cigar, lit it, and set it to his mouth.

"Boudica."

Boudica swatted away a fly that had landed on the top of her exposed tummy. "Captain," she offered, taking her time with each syllable, as she did with everything.

"Keeping cool?"

"Always."

It was a rare conversation where the Captain was the more active party. He disliked the role, though it was one he had anticipated playing when enlisting the opossum. "You busy?"

"Do I look it?"

"Up for some work?"

Boudica rose slowly from the dust of the creek bed. She brushed a layer of sand off her fur. "Hell, Captain," she said, her savage grin contrasting unpleasantly with the dreamy quietude of her eyes, "what took you so long?"

## Chapter 5

# Boudica's Arrival

When the Captain returned from the back Boudica was at the table, the brim of her sombrero covering most of her face. Leaning against the wall behind her was a rifle nearly as long as its owner, a black walnut stock with an intricately engraved barrel. She was smiling quietly at some jest of Bonsoir's as if she had been there all day—indeed, as if they had never parted.

He thought about saying something but decided against it.

## Chapter 6

# The Dragon's Lair

The Captain had been journeying for the better part of three days when he crested the woodland path into the clearing. He was in the north country, where there was still water, and trees, and green growing things—but even so it was a dry day, and the heat of the late afternoon held its grip against the coming of the evening. He was tired, and thirsty, and angry. Only the first two were remediable, or the results of his long walk. The inn was a squat, stone, two-story structure with a thatched roof and a low wall surrounding it. Above the entrance was a whittled sign that read EVERGREEN REST. Inside, a thin innkeeper waited to greet him, and a fat wife cooked stew, and a homely daughter set the tables.

The Captain did not go inside. The Captain swung around to the small garden that lay behind the building.

In recent years these sorts of hostelries had become less and less common, with bandits and petty marauders plaguing the roads, choking traffic, and making travel impossible for anyone unable to afford an armed escort. Even the lodges themselves had become targets, and those that remained had begun to resemble small forts, with high walls, and stout doors, and proprietors that greeted potential customers with cocked scatterguns.

The reason the Evergreen Rest had undergone no such revisions—the reason no desperado within five leagues was foolish enough to buy a glass of beer there, let alone make trouble—stood behind an old tree stump, an ax poised above his head. Age had withered his skin from a bright crimson to a deep maroon, but it had done nothing to excise the flecks of gold speckled through his flesh. Apart from the shift in hue, the years showed little on the salamander. He balanced comfortably on webbed feet, sleek muscle undiluted with blubber. His faded trousers were worn but neatly cared for. He had sweated through his white shirt and loosened his shoestring neck-tie to ease the passage of his breath.

He paused at the Captain's approach but went back to his work after a moment, splitting logs into kindling with sure, sharp motions. The Captain watched him dismember a choice selection of timber before speaking. "Hello, Cinnabar."

Cinnabar had calm eyes, friendly eyes, eyes that smiled and called you "sir" or "madam," depending on the case, eyes like cool water on a hot day. Cinnabar had hands that made corpses, lots of corpses, walls and stacks of them. Cinnabar's eyes never seemed to feel anything about what his hands did.

"Hello, Captain," Cinnabar's mouth said. Cinnabar's arms went back to chopping wood.

"It's been a while," the Captain added, as if he had just realized it.

"Time does that."

"Time does," the Captain agreed. "You surprised to see me?"

Cinnabar took another log from the pile, set it onto the tree stump. "Not really," he said, the denial punctuated by the fall of his ax.

The Captain nodded. It was not going well, he recognized, but he wasn't quite sure why or how to change it. He took his hat off and fanned himself for a moment before continuing. "You a cook?" While waiting for the answer he reached down and picked up a small rock.

"Busboy."

"It's been a long walk. Think I could get some water?"

Cinnabar stared at the Captain for a moment, as if searching for some deeper meaning. Then he nodded and started toward a rain barrel near the back entrance. As he did so the Captain, with a sudden display of speed, pitched the stone he had been holding at the back of his old companion's head.

For a stuttered second it sailed silently toward Cinnabar's skull. Then it was neatly cradled in the salamander's palm. But the motion that ought to have linked these two events—the causal bridge between them—was entirely absent, like frames cut from a film.

"That was childish," Cinnabar said, dropping the stone.

"I needed to see if you still had it."

Cinnabar stared at the Captain with his eyes that looked kind but were not.

"You know why I'm here?"

"Are you still so angry?"

The Captain drew himself up to his full height. It wasn't much of a height, but that was how high the Captain drew himself. "Yeah," he muttered. "Hell yeah."

Cinnabar turned his face back to the unchopped pile of wood. He didn't say anything.

Gradually the Captain deflated, his rage spent. "So you'll come?"

Cinnabar blinked once, slowly. "Yes."

The Captain nodded. The sound of someone laughing drifted out from the inn. The crickets took to chirruping. The two old friends stood silently in the fading light, though you wouldn't have known it to look at them. That they were old friends, I mean. Anyone could see it was getting dark.

## Chapter 7

# Cinnabar's Arrival

Cinnabar walked into the bar looking much the same as when the Captain had left him. A faded shirt, a black bolo tie threaded through it. But now he was weighted down with iron, as if afraid the southern wind might carry him away. Two oversized revolvers peeked out over his belt. The butt of a smaller cousin hung from his shoulder, a bulge in his boot rounding out the family reunion. Turning to hang his coat on the wall he revealed one final engine of destruction, a rifle with the barrel cut down. It was strapped sideways across his lower back, just above the root of his tail.

"Do you think you brought enough metal?" Bonsoir asked, whiskers twitching at the joke.

"For what we're planning?"

Bonsoir considered this for a moment before replying without any trace of his former good humor. "We should try to find you a shotgun."

Cinnabar nodded and took his seat.

## Chapter 8

# A Well-Earned Retirement

Barley was surprised to see a customer so late in the day. Since taking over the general store he had grown as familiar with the flow of commerce in his small town as a fisherman does with the current. It was a Sunday, and that meant a deluge of sales after church let out—penny candy and ribbons for the children, cask ale and bits of finery for their parents—but little enough thereafter. In fact he had planned to close early and head across the street to the town's only other establishment, a modest hostelry, drink a glass of cool beer and eat a steak dinner. He was glad now that he hadn't. Between the sun's glare and the weak eyes common to his species, he couldn't make out which of his regulars was standing in his doorway, but he waved him in anyway. He was a friendly sort, Barley. At least he had lately become so.

"Don't worry, we're open." His wide grin of greeting fell away as the Captain brushed through the entrance.

"Hello, Barley," the Captain said, extending his hand.

After a short but noticeable pause, Barley reached across the trestle and took it. "Captain." Barley was an adult badger, slate gray and nearly big enough to touch the ceiling. His palm was the size of the mouse's chest, and it swallowed up its counterpart as if hungry for more.

"It wasn't easy to find you."

"I didn't want to be found."

The Captain nodded and scanned the badger's establishment. It was spare but well maintained, rows of stock neatly arranged, the ground freshly swept. It was, in short, indistinguishable from a hundred other general stores the Captain had passed through in his lifetime. He tried to square it with his memories of the creature who managed it. It was hard going. "It's a nice place you've got."

Barley inspected the mouse's face for any hint of mockery. "Thanks. I took over a few years ago. The owner's daughter went east for work, and he didn't have anyone to leave it to."

"You like it?"

Barley smiled, almost self-consciously. "I do. It's . . . quiet. Since the mine dried up there's not much traffic. I know the customers; I know what they want. They come in smiling and they leave the same way."

The Captain nodded, not really listening. "I'm putting the old crew together."

"I'm out," Barley said. For years Barley had dreaded this moment, hoped it would never come, feared that when it did his courage would shrivel up and he wouldn't be able to cough out those words. The moment of truth had revealed itself as not being nearly so terrible as he had supposed. He decided to say it again. "I'm out. You've been good to me, Captain, but I've been good to you too. The way I figure it, we're even."

The Captain kept the off-white of his dead eye firm on the badger, but his face didn't twitch. "I need you, Barley. There's no one can do what you can do."

"What I do?" Barley smiled and nodded to his stock on the shelves behind him. "I sell things, Captain. Notepaper and spools of thread, frying pans and hardtack. You need any of those, I can give it to you at cost. But beyond that . . ." His lips drew into a frown and he shook his head slowly. "I don't kill anymore. I won't kill anymore. I'm through with it."

"We've all killed, Barley."

"Not like I have. Not so many, not near so many. None of you did, not even Cinnabar . . ." For a moment Barley's long snout hung open, and he lost himself in ugly memory. Then he blinked twice and turned back toward his chief. "I'm not arguing with you, Captain. I'm telling you how it is. I won't do it anymore. Everyone has the right to change."

The Captain nodded, unsurprised, but with a certain weary sadness. "I figured you'd say as much. I'm sorry."

"I'm sorry too . . ." Barley began, but before he could finish the Captain put furred fingers to his lips and let out a sharp whistle. The pair of sewer rats who entered then were as hard as pig iron, scarred things from one of the cities back east. The Captain had brought them special for the job. To judge by their kit and manner, it was not the first time they'd come to a foreign place for the purpose of doing evil.

Barley took a slow glance at the two of them, then turned his gaze back onto their employer. Having summoned his minions, the Captain now showed them a distinct lack of interest, his attention focused entirely on the badger.

The two rats were professionals, the first covering Barley with his rifle while the second fanned out to flank him, his hand on a big revolver dangling from his waist.

"This him?" the one with the rifle asked.

The Captain nodded.

The rat turned back to Barley. "Sorry, pal. Nothing personal."

"Just business," Barley agreed, his coal black eyes pinning down on the Captain.

The first rat nodded and leveled the rifle at Barley's skull; he was experienced enough to know one in the body wasn't a kill shot for a badger, not even at close range. He cocked the lever back. His partner stood by silently.

Badgers are not spry animals, and Barley was no outlier. But he understood the importance of committing to violence, of giving oneself over fully to savagery and not playing the flirt. And perhaps his placidity had lulled the rats into a false sense of security. Though well practiced in murder, they had misread his resignation—it was not acceptance of his own death that Barley's stillness signaled. It was acceptance of theirs.

Barley dropped suddenly to all fours, shielded briefly by the thick wood of the counter. There was a loud crack as a rifle bullet tore through the space the badger had just occupied. Then heavy splinters flew off in all directions, Barley pitching himself through the oak paneling and into his would-be assassin. The full weight of his shoulder impacted against the rat and bounced him against the side wall. A second crack, lower and softer than the retort of the rifle, signaled the shattering of the rodent's vertebrae.

The other rat managed to get a shot off, but his nerve was broken and he didn't take time to aim; the bullet tore a fat gouge from Barley's cheek but nothing more. He roared furiously and switched directions on a dime, his massive bulk flailing but his steps as graceful as a dancer's. The rat quivered his lower lip and squirted down his pant leg, and then Barley brought his hands together in a clap that shook the very foundations of the building.

Barley turned back to the Captain, mad with rage, his palms red with the outline of the slaughtered rat. He watched his old commander for a moment, the layers of tightly corded muscle and the fur surrounding it insufficient to contain his wild anger. Then he sprinted forward and scooped up the unresisting mouse with one hand, lifting him above the ground and giving him a shake that would have snapped the spine of a less hardy victim.

"Five years!" The Captain's whiskers were pinned back by the force of the roar. "Five years without murder, five years without a corpse! What have you done? What have you done?"

The Captain's face betrayed no knowledge that he was a few pounds per inch from oblivion, cool and steady and faintly mocking. "I made you a killer again."

Barley's eyes, as big as the Captain's head, bulged in their sockets. Barley's lip quivered in the sort of spasm of rage that often precedes murder.

But then Barley opened his grip, and the Captain fell awkwardly to the ground. He lay there for a half-moment, then pulled himself to his feet.

Barley face was sad and heavy. He stared at the wall as

though he was having trouble recognizing it.

"St. Martin's Day," the Captain said. "The Partisan's bar. Bring the machine."

After a long moment Barley nodded absently, and the Captain left, stepping casually over the broken body of the creature he had paid to die.

# Chapter 9

# Barley's Arrival

Given that he stretched perhaps triple the combined size of the creatures waiting for him, Barley managed to enter the bar without drawing undue attention to himself. It wasn't stealth, exactly; he was much too large for that. More a sort of unassuming quality that allowed eyes to pass over him without demanding the notice his dimensions rightfully demanded. In one hand he gripped the top handle of a black trunk, wide and presumably quite heavy, though you'd not have known it by the ease with which it was carried. Apart from whatever was inside, Barley had come unarmed.

The conversation at the back table had long since gone silent. The Captain was not one for small talk, even in his cups, and Boudica and Cinnabar's studied muteness made the mouse seem positively loquacious by comparison. Generally speaking, Bonsoir didn't see the silence of others as a barrier to conversation, but even the most committed orator requires some assistance from the chorus. Without it he had turned, like his companions, to the rewarding but largely silent task of getting drunk.

So Bonsoir looked up happily when the creaking floorboards indicated the arrival of another member of their merry band, and his smile widened as he discovered the newcomer's identity. Barley matched it with a grin that overran his snout and spilled over into a booming laugh. Unlikely as it seemed, the ink-black stoat and the broad-chested badger had been thick as thieves during their service, to use an overly sympathetic euphemism to describe years spent in the business of violence and mayhem.

"That's an ugly hat," Barley started.

Bonsoir's eyes went wide with mock fury. "This is the greatest hat anyone has ever worn," he said, pointing at his beret. "This hat was a a gift from the Emperor of Mexico, after I saved his life from a rampaging skunk. He begged me to stay on as his chief adviser, but I said, 'Emperor, Bonsoir cannot be caged, not even with bars of gold.'"

"Mexico doesn't have an emperor."

"That is Mexico's misfortune, for all of the greatest countries have emperors."

Barley laughed a second time and made his way to the oversized stool that Reconquista had put out to accommodate his ample backside. He set his case next to his chair and called for more liquor. From behind the counter the rat brought another jug to join its siblings scattered about the table.

If, as Barley had insisted, he had turned over a new leaf, and was no longer willing to countenance murder—he seemed altogether comfortable in the presence of creatures who had made it their calling.

## Chapter 10

# Our Old Friend, the Devil

The Captain slunk through the back streets of the Capital like waste through a drainage pipe. There were few enough now who could remember him, and the likelihood that any of them were spending this stormy evening in the slums north of the docks was slim—but the Captain was careful even when he didn't think he needed to be.

So he stuck to the shadows, and cut through alleys, and kept his hand firm on his revolver. The Captain did not like being in the Capital, had not been back since that grim final night five years past. But he had one more visit to make, one last strand to pull together, and it was not coincidence that he had saved it for last. The rain trickled down from the top of his hat to the brim, dripped over his dead eye and into his whiskers. It was the kind of storm that made walking feel like wading, the kind of rain that wet the ground without cooling the air. It was the right kind of weather for the business ahead. The Captain stifled a sniffle.

He took a turn down an unremarkable side street and stopped in front of a battered wooden house. No sign established it as a place of trade, and there was nothing to indicate it was anything but what it seemed; except the door was heavy, and thick, heavier and thicker than a door needed to be for a shack in a slum. The Captain banged on it, three solid blows.

A peephole slid open. A beady pair of eyes peeked out from it. "What you want?" a voice asked. It was not a friendly voice. Voices coming through peepholes rarely are.

"I'm here to see the Underground Man."

With most of his body obscured, it was an open question how exactly the gatekeeper responded to this piece of information. But the eyes, at least, clouded up with fear. "Who you be?"

"Someone who knows who to ask for."

The peephole slammed shut. The Captain heard the sound of a bolt unlocking, then the door opened to reveal a massive porcupine in a fine suit, perfectly tailored to allow for his prickly pines, any one of which was half again the size of the Captain.

"Welcome to the Setting Moon Café, sir. House policy requires all weapons be passed over for safekeeping." The bouncer's thick patois had been replaced with an upscale accent, but a quiver broke through it, as if the mention of the Underground Man was an invocation sufficient to unsettle him.

The Captain handed over his revolver. It represented perhaps a solid quarter of his armaments, though if the porcupine realized this he was wise enough not to make it an issue. "Speak to the bartender, sir, about your business," he said, then, breaking role suddenly, he set a hand on the Captain's arm. "If you're certain you want to be about it."

The Captain shook off the porcupine's grip and descended the stairs without responding.

It would have come as a surprise to the homeless and destitute creatures who eked out a miserable existence on the streets above that their block—indeed, the neighborhood—was little more than camouflage, rough casing for the subterranean organs below. Beneath the boarded-up row houses was a sprawling citadel of sin, decadent and opulent, beautiful and corrupt. Scantily clad females carried trays of liquor to powerful males, threading their way through poker tables and roulette wheels. In one corner was a stage, though at the moment it was vacant of any entertainment. In another a door led to a suite of back rooms, and the pleasures on offer there were always available, so long as you had coin to pay.

The Captain paid no attention to the decor, or the females, or their clientele. The Captain was singular in his single-mindedness. He took an empty stool at the back counter, far away from the few packs of revelers, and he waved down the bartender.

"Whiskey? Smoke? Something more satisfying?"

"I'll take the first," the Captain said, pulling a cigar from a pocket and lighting it. "And I've got the second."

"How about the third?" the bartender asked with practiced charm.

The straight line of the Captain's mouth didn't waver. "I'm here to see the Underground Man."

The bartender went wide-eyed and threw back the shot of whiskey he had just poured for the Captain. "She knows you're coming?"

"Who knows what the Underground Man knows?"

"Who indeed?" The bartender poured himself another glass and drank that as well. "I'll let her know you're here. If she don't wanna see you..." The bartender shrugged. "You probably won't be seen again."

The Captain didn't seem impressed by that. The bartender disappeared into a back door.

It was a slow night or the guinea pig probably wouldn't have bothered. The Captain did not seem desperate for company, though on the other hand, company was usually the reason animals made their way to the Setting Moon Café. So she sidled two seats over, drawing the Captain's attention with her ample bulk.

"Not interested," he said flatly.

She smiled. She was pretty, for a guinea pig, if you didn't mind them heavy. If you did mind them heavy you probably wouldn't go for a guinea pig. "Slow down a minute, sugar. No one's asking for a ring. How about you just buy me a drink?"

"I'm not paying for this one," the Captain said. "I could not pay for another." He reached over the bar and grabbed a glass, then filled it from the bottle before sliding it to her. He had to stretch.

She recognized his courtesy with a quick bob of her head, then took a sip of her drink. Time passed. She fluttered her eyelashes and offered a coquettish smile. But the Captain's shallow reserve of gentility was depleted, and he ignored the bait.

She decided to go for broke. "I could put a smile on your face," she whispered, running the pink of her tail down the Captain's leg.

"No, you couldn't," he said, and his one good eye didn't look at her.

Another moment beside his ground-glass scowl and she decided he was probably right. As her hope for a transaction evaporated her demeanor changed, leavened into something more natural. "What're you here for then?"

The Captain rolled a few fingers of liquor down the recess of his throat. "I'm here to see the devil."

A flicker of fear, though she hid it swiftly. "I'm not sure I know him, stranger."

The Captain poured another charge into his cup, disposed of it with one neat motion. "Everybody knows the devil. But not everyone works for her."

The guinea pig swallowed hard. "I don't know anything about that, stranger. I stick to my own business."

Now the Captain did smile, though she found she wished he hadn't. "Let's hope that's enough to save you."

The bartender came out from the back then, shaking his head in wonder or fear. "She'll see you, stranger," he began. "Follow that passage to the end." He opened his mouth as if to say something else, perhaps to try to dissuade the Captain, but in the end he remained silent. The mouse did not look like the sort of creature who left a place with his aims unfulfilled. And besides, security had already marked him. One way or the other, he was going to see the Underground Man. The open question was whether he'd come back out again.

The Captain slid off his stool and walked into the back, without a word of thanks or farewell for the bartender or his erstwhile companion. The door led to a long corridor, and then to a second door, grim and featureless. He banged his tiny fist against the wood. It opened almost immediately, the dour rats behind it apprised of the Captain's arrival.

Rats are not, generally speaking, friendly creatures, but even by the standard of their species the small plague rats were particularly menacing. They did, however, up-end the age-old species stereotype of being unhygienic and ill-disciplined, in fact exhibiting a neat uniformity in dress and manner, clad in well-fitting black fatigues and scowls to match the Captain's own. Or nearly, at least; the Captain was a hell of a scowler.

This time the search was thorough, and the Captain ended it without his irons or much of his dignity. The former concerned him more than the latter.

Two of the rats hustled the Captain down another wandering corridor, spending a long few minutes in silence. They were thorough professionals, and the knowledge that they might well find themselves firing their shouldered scatterguns at the mouse's back precluded any misplaced cordiality. For his part, the Captain just didn't like talking.

They came to a final door, ebony accented in rosewood, a centered doorknob of sterling silver. "She's ahead of you," one of the rats ventured. "And we're behind."

If the Captain felt any way about this, you couldn't have told from his face. He opened the door and stepped inside.

The Underground Man's sanctuary was a towering cylindrical chamber, as dissimilar to the rest of the Setting Moon Café as the Setting Moon Café was to the surrounding neighborhood. Its defining feature was the bookshelves that wrapped around the walls, housing thousands upon thousands of leather-bound volumes, a rolling ladder offering access to their wisdom. At floor level the concentric circles of an Oriental rug strangled a jet-black desk. A single gas lamp dangled down from a long chain attached to the distant ceiling. There was a small door opposite the one the Captain had just come through, which led, presumably, into the owner's sleeping quarters.

In the center of this vast edifice of erudition, surrounded by a ring of the most jaded debauchery, encompassed finally by abject poverty, stood a fat mole in Eastern pajamas. She took a few steps toward the Captain, her blind eyes twinkling through bifocals. Her hands were crossed inside her wide sleeves. Her pink snout quivered in the air, inspecting the new arrival. Behind the Captain the guards fingered their weapons, prepping for the kill.

"My old friend," the Underground Man said, extending her hand. "My dear old friend."

The Captain took it. "Gertrude." He nodded to the books, or perhaps to the building that surrounded them. "You've done well for yourself."

Gertrude shrugged self-effacingly at the surrounding splendor. "One has to keep busy. And you? How have you occupied the last half-decade?"

"I joined a nunnery."

"Here soliciting donations?"

"Not exactly."

"No, I imagined not. Now would be the time—the Capital rots, the country boils, the roads are awash in banditry and disorder." She scratched her chin, settled her arms around a rotund belly. "Have you thought about how you'll do it?"

"Yes."

"Loquacious as ever." Gertrude burped a laugh. "I assume it begins with the Elder."

The Captain grunted.

"He should be easy enough to find. And if you've got everyone together, easy enough to get. But what happens after?"

The Captain shrugged. A silent moment dripped away. "I figured that was where you came in."

"I suppose I might be of some assistance. Though that does raise another issue." She went to the bar on her desk, filled two glasses with a golden liquid trapped in an opaque decanter, turned, and handed one to her guest. "What's in it for me?"

The Captain sipped his drink, but above it his eyes

didn't leave the mole. "You could be the Lady of the Manor."

"I couldn't. And besides, I don't want to be Lady."

"Me, neither. But I wouldn't mind whispering in her ear."

"You say that, but I'm not sure I believe you." Gertrude drained a few fingers of alcohol through her long snout. "At the bottom, I think there's nothing in this for you but blood."

"So what do you want?" the Captain asked testily. He was not a fellow who enjoyed having his mind probed.

Gertrude gestured casually at her surroundings, opulence flavored with refinement. "I have it. What we had hoped to gain collectively, I've taken on my own."

"Would you do it for the sake of old times?"

"I rather think not. We are creatures little troubled by such extravagances as loyalty—and even still, your probable suicide mission would be stretching the bonds."

"Then do it because we're going to go for it whether you throw your hand in or not. If you stay out of it, and it goes our way, then you'll be left in the cold. And if you stay out of it, and we fail . . . I imagine you might experience a brief twinge of regret."

Gertrude smirked. "Very brief."

A few more seconds drifted by, then Gertrude sighed and made a motion dismissing her guards. "It would be nice to see the Dragon again," she admitted. "And of course, there is that lingering question of who exactly betrayed us."

"I've been wondering about that myself," the Captain said, his visage more than usually terrible.

# Chapter 11

# Gertrude's Arrival

Gertrude came in through the back door, looking very little like the criminal despot the Captain had spoken to some three weeks earlier. She had swapped her Eastern garb for a faded calico dress, homespun and homely.

Cinnabar leaned over to the Captain. "That's everyone, then?"

"Not quite."

# Chapter 12

# Elf

The crew was arguing. The crew spent a lot of time arguing.

"It was Harelip and Half-Eye Pete. How do you think he got that half-eye?" Barley asked.

"I had always assumed he was born with it," Bonsoir said.

"You thought he was born with a knife scar running from his forehead to his lip?"

Bonsoir shrugged and made a popping sound with his mouth. "It was not an issue I felt compelled to contemplate."

"We worked with them for two years," Gertrude insisted. "How could you not have known they were lovers? Or that, when they stopped being lovers, Harelip cut out half of Half-Eye Pete's eye?"

"Hello, friends," interrupted the creature who appeared then from the darkness.

Cinnabar had a revolver out and cocked almost instantaneously, and a second thereafter Bonsoir kicked his chair from beneath him and came up with a length of steel. Gertrude shifted behind Barley, who had assumed his full height menacingly, and Boudica went for the holdout piece she kept in her boot.

Only the Captain remained in his chair, unruffled, sipping from his jug. "Hello, Elf."

Elf was small for an owl, barely taller than Bonsoir. Her feathers, once smooth and tawny, had grown mottled and spare with age, but the cold horn of her beak seemed keen as ever. Her eyes were sulfur-yellow and wide as saucers, and they seemed not to blink, nor even to shudder. She stood indifferently on talons sharp as the scorn of a lover, the weight of her body tilted with curious asymmetry. Some earlier injury had shattered the bone of her left wing, and it curled up against her body and contorted her posture.

A long moment slipped past as the crew resumed their resting positions. Once seated, they did not fall over themselves in excitement to greet the new arrival. Cinnabar nodded. Barley allowed himself a brief grunt.

It is generally not possible to determine, from their expression alone, what a bird is feeling—a beak can tear, rend, or peck, but it cannot smile or frown—so it is possible that Elf was terribly offended by this lackadaisical welcome, and simply unable to show it. It seems unlikely, however.

"Why don't you have yourself a seat?" the Captain asked. "Reconquista can find you something to drink."

There was something very much like a collective gasp of discomfort from the seated assemblage.

"No, thank you, Captain," Elf responded in her quiet monotone. "The trip here was long, and I much prefer the stars." She ducked her head in a nod, once to the mouse, once to the rest of the group, then turned toward the door. Belaying the utter quiet of her approach, her exit was loud and slow, claws rapping against wood. "Oh, Captain," Elf began again, head swiveling backward, "if the rat might find a bowl of milk for me, I would be grateful."

"Of course," the Captain responded amiably. "I'll have it sent right out."

Elf nodded the full moon of her backward face, then swung it forward and hobbled out into the night. The silence filled with apprehension.

"God of the Gardens, Captain, what the hell is she doing here?"

"We'll need her before the end."

"I was sure she was dead."

"She can't even scout for us anymore, with that wing."

The Captain growled, more of a squeak really, but it had the same effect. "We'll need her before the end."

The crowd quieted and turned back to their drinks. The Captain had given the word, and if you didn't trust the Captain to take care of his end, then there wasn't any point in being there. But still, no one looked happy.

# Chapter 13

# The Plan

"So that's the plan," the Captain said, although actually it was only part of it.

Boudica took her hat off, looked at it a while, then put it back on her head. Gertrude twittered her snout. Cinnabar smoked a cigarette.

"What about when it's over?" Barley asked. "What do we do then?"

Bonsoir chittered suddenly, his oblong body shaking with mirth. "'When it's over?' He laughed again, louder and longer, till his fur stood on end; he seemed convulsed with glee. "We are planning on facing the entire might of the Gardens with only the seven of us, and you are worried about your soft retirement? Do not worry, my friend, we won't be around to enjoy it!"

The good humor spread back to Barley, who smiled sheepishly. Gertrude offered her meaningless little smirk, and Boudica was grinning anyway. Lizards don't exactly have lips, but Cinnabar seemed vaguely happy all the same. Even the Captain smiled.

Sort of. It was close. It counted for the Captain.

## Chapter 14

# Later . . .

"What happened to the Captain's eye?" Bonsoir asked Barley while getting steadily drunk in the corner.

"That day when—"

"What day?"

"That day."

"Oh. *That* day."

"Yeah. Anyway. Remember Alfalfa the hare? Said pistols bored him, liked to do his work with dynamite?"

"Sure. He still owes me money."

"I wouldn't expect to collect. Mephetic turned him, I dunno how. Once the trouble started he lit one of those boom sticks. Captain put him down, but . . ." Barley shrugged his swelled shoulders. "Not fast enough. The explosion took out the Captain's eye, and it did for that half of Reconquista that isn't there anymore."

"I always liked that half."

"I imagine Reconquista was partial to it as well."

# Chapter 15

# And Later . . .

"I don't remember her being so crazy," Bonsoir began. Bonsoir often began things wiser members of the company preferred to leave sleeping.

"She was always off," Barley said. Slurred, really.

"She was always off, but she was not always like this."

"You can't trust a bird."

"You can't trust anyone."

"She took the betrayal hard."

"I didn't like it any more than she did," Bonsoir responded. "But I didn't let it drive me mad either."

"You didn't lose your arm," Barley growled.

"It's not the wound," Gertrude chimed in. "It's the one who made it."

"You mean the Quaker?" This from Bonsoir.

"Can you remember how they used to be together? They refused to be separated. Not in camp or on a job, not sleeping or waking. When Elf toileted, he used to coil outside."

"I remember."

"One thing to be betrayed by a friend. Another entirely to be betrayed by a lover."

"Wasn't that either," Cinnabar piped in. His chair was tilted backward, his legs up on the table. "It's the ground."

Bonsoir looked confused. "The ground?"

"She wasn't meant for it. She's a flyer, and she's spent the last five years hobbling." The brim of Cinnabar's hat still covered his eyes. "That would drive anything crazy."

# Chapter 16

# And Yet Later . . .

The Captain had just finished marking his territory when a shadow hooted greeting. He buttoned unstained trousers and turned to face her. "Well?"

"He will be there?"

"He'll be there."

"You're certain?" Elf's eyes were bright, and between them and the moon there seemed no distinction in circumference. "You're certain?"

The Captain was not honest, exactly, as many a creature had learned to its despair. But the Captain had a word, and once that word was given one did not question it, not even if one was Elf.

"Excuse me," she said, turning away from his scowl. "It's just that I've so longed to see him." Her malformed wing shuddered against her torso. "I've just longed to see him so."

When the Captain walked back into the bar, the rest of them assumed he was only unsteady with drink.

# Chapter 17

# And Later Still . . .

The rows of empty jugs had multiplied with the speed of caged rabbits. They piled onto the table and flowed over onto the ground. They were stacked high in the corner. They rolled out the back door.

"Down with the false lord!" Reconquista shrieked suddenly. "Long live the Elder! Long live the true Lord of the Manor!"

Bonsoir borrowed a pistol from Cinnabar and fired into the air. Barley beat his chest as if to break a rib. Boudica hooted once then fell silent. Drunk as they were, they'd have cheered for the moon to make war on the stars, and offered odds on the result.

## Chapter 18

# So Late as to Be Early . . .

Morning had begun its assumption over evening. The fire was long gray, no one left awake interested in tending it. In the corner Bonsoir and Barley had fallen asleep leaning against each other. The stoat had one arm around his old friend and the other coiled protectively over a jug of liquor. The badger snored loudly enough to awaken anyone not in a drunken stupor. Happily this was exactly how Boudica found herself, passed out behind the counter. Gertrude and Cinnabar were still at the table, drinking quietly. The Captain was nowhere to be seen.

Reconquista's bar had seen better days, though the rat himself, collapsed on the back porch, didn't seem to mind. Most of the windowpanes were unbroken. No permanent structural damage had been done. There weren't any corpses to dispose of. Still, the bartender would have work to do when he woke, shattered jugs and empty bottles and overturned chairs and overturned tables and green stains on the walls and brown stains on the floors, both emitting odors that, as a rule, were best confined to an outhouse.

"Funny thing about it," Cinnabar began softly, "I didn't like the Elder."

"I could never tell one from the other," Gertrude admitted.

# Chapter 19

# The Power Behind the Throne

Mephetic had just left his office when the messenger arrived, and he was in an off mood. He was often in an off mood these days, weighed down by the endless bureaucratic details involved in being High Chancellor—grain harvests, floundering tax revenue, banditry, relations with neighboring kingdoms. When he'd organized the coup that had deposed the Captain and his pet claimant five years earlier, he had imagined his life involving more drunken bacchanals and fewer hours double-checking the sums of petty functionaries. Owning the crown, Mephetic had discovered—or, more accurately, owning the creature who owned it—was not all it was cracked up to be. Needless to say, the toad himself was no help. Most of the time he was barely awake.

So perhaps it was understandable that Mephetic's first reaction upon discovering that his old nemesis was not only still alive but actively working toward his downfall was not fear, or anger, or even anxiety—it was outright excitement. He clutched the letter to his breast, and a slow smile stretched across his jaws. He hadn't expected he'd ever need to make use of the traitor again, but he'd been paying him a bit by way of upkeep, just in case of this eventuality. The Captain's body had never been found, after all. When he threw the last handful of dirt on the mouse's coffin, then he'd be certain. Not before.

On his way to the cellars Mephetic caught himself in a mirror, spent a moment reflecting on his reflection, and decided he was not displeased. It had been years since there was a challenge to his position, and years before that since any wetwork had been required of him; most days he didn't even bother to carry a gun. But he had kept in shape—the mask of his face was still a vibrant black, and his reek was sharp as old cheese. He nodded to himself. If the mouse was coming, he'd find a fit adversary.

More than one in fact, Mephetic thought as he headed toward the officer's mess.

A long walk (the castle was a large place) found the skunk in one of the many sumptuous quarters of the vast estate: walls with bright watercolor murals, antique furniture, bottles strewn over the floor. Brontë reclined on some couches in one corner. A sleek, handsome fox, her fur bright red with fetching streaks of white, her claws neat and sharp and clean. Above her forehead was pinned a bright purple ribbon. Leaning against the wall behind her was a double-barreled blunderbuss, filigreed and shaped to fit her paw. For a smaller creature it would have been a shotgun, but for Brontë it functioned effectively enough as a pistol. It was a lovely looking thing, and Brontë liked using it whenever appropriate, and in a good number of situations where it strictly speaking wasn't.

Next to her a calico cat puffed away at a hubble-bubble. Puss's watch cost more than his vest, and his vest cost more than his boots, and his boots cost more than a house. If you stripped him naked and sold off his costume, you'd walk away with enough money to retire—though if you left him alive you wouldn't have long to enjoy it. The only thing that could rival Puss's vanity was his sadism.

Puss was rough and Brontë was worse, though as far as Mephetic was concerned neither could hold a candle, in terms of sheer menace, to the last member of the trio, coiled tightly against the back wall. They were his top ranks, the troubleshooters who helped to keep the Gardens running, any one of the three as dangerous as a battalion of rat guard. And if they didn't quite snap to attention when Mephetic came through the door, well, they weren't exactly your run-of-the-mill grunts, now were they? And they knew enough at least to pay him his due. Mephetic hadn't gotten to where he was by being made of tissue paper.

He laid the situation out for them quickly, with little preamble and no aggrandizement.

"Well welcomed, as far as I'm concerned," Puss said. Puss had drawing-room manners, and he was as amoral as a loaded gun. "I haven't had anything interesting to do since coming to this backwater hellhole."

"Not up to the standards of the Old Country?" Brontë asked.

"Nothing is," Puss said, doffing his hat regretfully. "Would that father had been willing to overlook my . . . youthful indiscretions."

"Which indiscretions were those? Dueling or buggery?"

Puss mulled this over for a moment. "You know, I can't quite remember."

Puss and Brontë laughed merrily. They were the best of friends. One of them was likely to kill the other before long.

Brontë turned to face the third of Mephetic's high commanders. "You worked with them," she said. "What can we expect?"

The Quaker had fed recently; you could tell from the fat knot stuck midway down his coil. This was the only reason Brontë had been willing to speak with him, and even so she asked the question from across the room, out of the serpent's effective range, or so she hoped. The

Quaker's head was perched atop the tight weave of his body, and for a long moment it seemed he had not heard the question or simply didn't care to answer. But then his ghost-white tail began to rattle, like rain falling against a windowpane, though far less comforting.

Mephetic nodded to himself. He was ready for the Captain.

# PART THE SECOND

## Chapter 20

# South of the Border

Angie Weasel was drinking from the trough. She righted herself and blinked twice. It was a hot day, sun beating off dust as far as you'd want to look, and a creature could get to seeing things that weren't there. She squinted and fanned herself with her hat. She called to Bessie Weasel, her younger sister, slung out on the swinging bench that hung from the roof of the patio, just outside the main house. It was the only structure that remained standing, apart from a large barn rotting a few hundred paces to her rear. Bessie sighed. Bessie listened to the hinges squeal. By the time Bessie had managed to stand several minutes had passed, and the Captain and Cinnabar were clearly within view, and so her effort was altogether wasted.

A brief word on weasels—it is not a coincidence that their species has entered the popular nomenclature as synonym for duplicity and cheapness of character. No one has ever caressed a lover and said, "You weasel." A mother does not call her babe a "weasel" as she brings it to breast. A weeping son does not eulogize his newly dead father as "my dearest weasel." As a rule, they exemplify the sort of low cunning and brute force that is little in demand among the civilized creatures of the world.

The Weasel sisters were very much emblematic of the species, if perhaps slightly nastier than the norm. They had come down from the Gardens years ago, just ahead of a mob of animals looking to hang them by their long necks. With such qualifications, they'd had no trouble finding work in the Kingdom to the South. The Kingdom to the South was that sort of a place.

It was a long time before the two of them came within speaking distance. The Captain wasn't the hurrying kind. Cinnabar, though he could move very fast, very fast indeed, was not the hurrying kind either. The Weasel sisters were also not much for haste, or at least they didn't snap to attention at the arrival of their guests; they didn't even bother with a greeting.

"You gonna tell your boss we're here?" the Captain asked.

Angie Weasel walked over and banged on the door of the house.

"You must be the Dragon," Bessie Weasel said.

Cinnabar didn't respond.

"You don't look like no dragon to me."

"You ever seen a dragon?" the Captain asked.

"No."

"Then your opinion don't hold much weight."

Angie Weasel snickered. Bessie Weasel scowled. Things might have gone bad right then if the door hadn't opened, and the only creature alive who could control the Weasel sisters came out of it.

It had been years since the Captain had seen Zapata, but he looked exactly the same. Armadillos age slowly, after all. The plate of their armor grows thicker and denser, gray scales shielding the soft flesh beneath. But apart from that there is little enough to distinguish a pup from an elder. A pair of bandoliers crisscrossed his wide chest and two fat revolvers peeked up from his belt. A sombrero, turned off-white by long years in the sun, shaded the narrow point of his face. Zapata gave the simultaneous impression of a tyrant and clown, like he would make you laugh before having you shot.

He approached the Captain with an excitement one sees in lovers long separated, his claws outstretched as if for an embrace. When he saw the Captain wasn't going to go for it he shortened his paws up to at least offer a handshake. When he saw the Captain wasn't going to go for that either he set them into his pockets. He remained smiling, however. "The Captain himself! The Elder's avenger, bringer of righteous death! How long has it been, my friend?"

" A while."

"And by his side the Dragon, just as in the old days!"

Cinnabar nodded but didn't say anything.

"You are both welcome, and more than welcome, to my humble abode. But perhaps this conversation is best done away from any prying eyes?" Zapata waved toward the entrance.

The Captain looked at Cinnabar. What passed between them, none could justly say. Then the Captain followed Zapata indoors, Cinnabar holding his spot by the trough.

Only the front room of the house remained usable, the rest having long fallen into disrepair, overgrown by the scrub grass that was the only form of flora the desert allowed. There was a table, and two chairs, and one rat who closed the door after the Captain had come inside. Zapata took a seat and waited for the Captain to take the other. For a moment it looked like he intended to stand, but then he gave the guard a glance that would have curdled milk and dropped down across from Zapata.

"I must say," the armadillo began, unplugging the cork from a jug resting beside him and taking a swig, "I was surprised when you contacted me." He pushed the liquor across the wood.

The Captain eyed it for a moment, then pushed it back. "Because you thought I was dead?"

When Zapata laughed, his stomach rocked the table back and forth. "Please now, Captain, we both know you're too ornery to die. Though to judge by your eye, Mephetic took a pretty good run at it. How did that happen, exactly? One moment you are cock of the walk, and the next your throat is all but cut."

"I suppose I'm just too trusting."

Zapata laughed again. Zapata laughed often. "It is your one failing, if you don't mind me saying so! You're too trusting."

The Captain's appetite for humor had been well and fully satisfied by this point, however, and he refused to continue the jest. Zapata took another pull from the jug, then plugged it and set it back on the table. "Well, Captain, as far as I am concerned, it was worth the trip out here simply to see you. But I imagine you had a purpose in contacting me."

"I need to find the Elder."

Zapata pulled at the roots of his long mustache. "Why would I know where your old patron resides?"

"I know he fled to the south after everything went sour. And it would be in your country's interest to keep him alive. You've got the connections with the new government to know where he is. And besides—there aren't so many folks left from the old days to call on."

Zapata nodded, as if the Captain's last words contained some great weight of profundity. "That is true, Captain, that is very true. There are few enough of us alive who can still remember the war. Why do you think that is?"

"It's a dangerous world."

"You misunderstand—I am not asking why you think so many have fallen. I'm asking you why you think I've survived."

"I guess it's because you're so damned good looking," the Captain said, though he seemed unamused with his joke.

Zapata, by contrast, slapped his hands against his knees and roared with laughter. "I had forgotten how funny you were, Captain. But no, that is not why. The reason I have survived is very simple—it is because I am a survivor."

"And I'm not?"

"No, Captain, I do not think you are. Don't misunderstand me—you survive, obviously, or we wouldn't be talking right now. But I do not think you are a survivor, if you see the difference."

"I imagine it's about to be explained."

"You see, my old friend—I do what needs to be done at the moment I need to do it, and I don't concern myself overmuch with the day before or after. When the Kingdom to the South looked weak, I raised the flag of rebellion. When it grew stronger, I made peace, and reaped the rewards. The wind blows, and I let it carry me along. Not you—quite the opposite, really. You find the fiercest gale you can and spit into its face! Now one might admire your audacity, and even the strength it takes to stand your comeuppance. But still, the wind blows, does it not? And you . . . you are still wet."

The Captain nodded vaguely. "Thanks for the advice."

Zapata smiled, laughed, scratched himself, slapped the table, took up a lot of space and attention. Somewhere in the midst of his buffoonery he shot his rat a look that he didn't intend the Captain to see.

The mouse is a curious animal. He is small and weak. If he is not slow, he is slower than the cat, the fox, and the owl, his natural predators—which is to say he is not nearly fast enough. His claws and teeth are fragile things, unsuited to violence. Generally speaking he cannot even blend in to his surroundings. In short, the mouse is perhaps the single most helpless animal on earth, blessed with nary a resource to defend himself against the cruel privations of a savage world.

Save one—the mouse knows it. The mouse is too feeble to cling to any illusions of safety. From the instant he leaves the flesh of the womb, he knows his life is there for the taking, and he grows cagey, and sharp. He sees the goshawk above him, sniffs out the polecat lurking in the shadows.

All of which is to say that when the rat leveled his sawed-off shotgun the Captain was already moving, kicking his chair backward and falling with it, the load of buckshot passing swiftly through the space he had occupied and nestling itself into Zapata's ripe and unsuspecting chest. The Captain had meanwhile shaken a hold-out pistol from the sleeve of his coat, and he used the first two of its chambers to make sure his would-be assassin would not have time to regret the mistake. The rat staggered into a corner, counting down its last breaths. The Captain turned his weapon on Zapata, though he realized swiftly that the armadillo no longer presented a threat.

The Captain came slowly to his feet. He picked up his hat from where it had fallen and set it onto his head, his ears flattening to hold it upright. He returned his pistol to his sleeve holster.

From outside there were a series of gunshots, coming so swiftly it was impossible to make out the number.

The spray of lead had ripped through Zapata's underbelly. His intestines were leaking into a little puddle on the floor, blood and bile with them. He smiled all the same. "That'll be my girls."

The Captain pulled a stool in front of Zapata and sat down atop it. The air erupted with a cavalcade of gunfire, rendering conversation inaudible.

After thirty seconds or so the artillery ended. The Captain slipped a cigar from his pocket, lit it, and took a few shallow draws. "You sure?"

# Chapter 21

# A Killer's Pride

"I will be honest with you, my old friend—this whole thing is wounding my ego."

Bonsoir was pacing back and forth on a dune a long ways off from the hacienda, the jet-black of his fur standing out against the pink sand.

"I hear ya," Boudica grunted. She lay motionless just beneath the crest of the hill, gray fur stained to dull khaki by the dust. From twenty paces away she was absolutely indistinguishable from the sediment surrounding her—save for the long, glittering barrel of her rifle. It was an unnecessary obfuscation, in all likelihood. They were too far from the meeting place to be seen unaided, a fact that explained Bonsoir's distinct lack of stealth. But Boudica was a professional, and professionalism means doing it right even when it doesn't matter.

"Bonsoir is the greatest infiltration specialist in history. Bonsoir is as slippery as moonlight, as slick as shade and as swift as sin."

"No question."

"And what is Bonsoir doing, with all his talent? With his ability that no one, not Bonsoir's worst enemies—not that Bonsoir leaves so many of those alive to have an opinion one way or the other on the matter, needless to say—but still, if one was up above the ground, and you were to ask him, 'Bonsoir, is he everything they say he is,' this theoretical enemy would be heard to answer, 'Yes, without question.' What was I saying?"

"Not sure."

Bonsoir paused for a moment. "The point is, this is a misuse of my genius."

"Captain's got his plan."

"Indeed he does! And the Captain, he says he does not need Bonsoir today! He says that today is not Bonsoir's! That you and the lizard will take care of the ones outside, and that Barley and his cannon will take care of the ones in the barn, and so there is nothing left for Bonsoir." Bonsoir scowled and kicked at the dirt.

"It's tough."

"The indignity!" Bonsoir said, sticking one finger straight up in the air. "It is an insult to my ability, that's what it is! A disgrace to my line and lineage, to my people and nation and . . ."

Bonsoir would almost certainly have continued on in this fashion had not the retort of the rifle cut him off.

"Did you get her?" Bonsoir asked.

Boudica looked up from the weapon with a pained expression.

"I'm sorry, I'm sorry. You can see how out of sorts this whole thing has made me."

"You'll get your turn soon enough."

# Chapter 22

# The Price of Certainty

"I've heard about you," Angie Weasel said. Slyly, as if betraying a secret.

This news did not seem to excite Cinnabar. His eyes hung dully on the closed door of the hacienda, as if hoping to follow his commander through the rough stone.

"I guess everyone's heard about you."

The shuttered window on the second floor of the hacienda peeked open, and Celia Weasel, the youngest of the clan, leaned the barrel of her Winchester out of it. It was an ominous sign, one Cinnabar gave no indication of noticing.

"Is it true you killed High-Hand Lawrence and Hot-pants the squirrel during the same card game?"

Nothing from Cinnabar. No words, no change in his demeanor, no breathing, only the absolute stillness of which only a cold-blooded creature is capable.

"I wonder if you're as fast as they say," Bessie Weasel chirruped, her hand slowly straying toward her belt.

"Wondering is free," Cinnabar said finally, his voice soft and low. "Certainty has its price."

The blast from inside was the signal. Angie Weasel went for her iron with all the speed and vigor possessed by a member of her race. Bessie Weasel was only a hairsbreadth slower in swiveling her shotgun. Celia Weasel was caught off guard but responded with a reasonable degree of alacrity all the same.

It is a scientific fact that time is infinitely divisible, that each moment contains within it the fragments of a thousand others, and each of them can be splintered into a thousand more, and so on and so on. Somewhere then, hidden within these shards of time that occur in the endless instants between the second hand, Cinnabar moved, setting his webbed palm around the pistol at his waist and fanning off two shots. To the subjective observer, however—to Angie and her unfortunate sibling—the salamander's movements were impossible to follow. Before their brains could process the information gathered by their senses, perhaps even before their senses had recognized the stimulus itself, bits of iron had exploded through their skulls and made either act impossible.

Celia might have had a chance. Maybe. She was good, and Cinnabar was only flesh. But as she tightened her finger a shot rang out in the distance, and then the youngest Weasel sister was tumbling out the window, dead before she struck the ground.

Cinnabar slipped his gun back into his holster. He waved at Boudica, or where he assumed Boudica to be. His eyes studied the horizon, open and friendly.

# Chapter 23

# A Loud Death Rattle

A hundred and fifty paces behind the barn a small, pink ball broke through the packed dust of the earth, rising half an inch and hovering for a moment before withdrawing. A few seconds passed and the tip of Gertrude's nose was joined by the rest of her. She turned quickly and widened out the exit, allowing her much larger companion to join her aboveground.

Barley stretched to his full height, enjoying the feel of his spine snapping back into place. Then he reached into the hole and withdrew a large black trunk, quite the size of Gertrude herself and, to judge by the grunt the badger gave while lifting it, not filled with feathers.

Her task completed, Gertrude set to brushing off the grime and dirt that had accumulated during her sojourn beneath the soil. It was an impossible task, but it occupied her time. "I speak seven languages, did you know that?"

Barley undid the latch on his chest. "I'll take your

word for it." He opened the trunk, pulled out a tarp, and laid it on the ground beside him. Then he began to remove any number of strange metallic bits, pipes and cylinders and gleaming silver cogs. He inspected each carefully before lining them up on the canvas.

"Seven languages," Gertrude confirmed. "My knowledge of mathematics, literature, law, philosophy, poisons, explosives, and espionage are, I think I do myself no exaggerated kindness in saying, second to no one still living within the Gardens."

"You're very clever," Barley agreed. Having ensured that his inventory was complete, he had turned toward its assembly, hands steady, movement swift. "Everyone thinks so."

"And the first thing he has me do—the very first thing—is dig a hole."

"What can you say?" he slammed the last piece into place and stood upright, revealing the engine of destruction he had spent the last few moments building. "It's in our blood."

The organ gun was eight wide barrels rotating around a self-feeding cartridge belt. During the War of the Two Brothers the Captain had purchased a handful of them from back east, but they had proved too heavy and unwieldy to be used effectively. Three animals were generally required to operate one gun, and even then it was hard to move, and likely to jam, and only any good for holding a position.

Barley lifted it up against his chest with a low grunt. He strapped the attached pack of ammo to his back.

"You still using that absurd contraption?" Gertrude asked, packing an ash-wood pipe with a tuft of fragrant tobacco.

"No."

Gertrude rolled her blind eyes mockingly. "A figment of my imagination."

Somewhere ahead of them, hidden by the barn itself, was the crack of a scattergun, followed by another series of shots. The barn door opened suddenly and a rat burst out of it, rifle in hand, a stream of comrades close on his heels.

Barley waited for the first wave to make it out the exit before he started on his hand crank. The years of inactivity had done nothing to diminish the gun's efficacy, nor the gunner's expertise. For a full half-minute nothing could be heard over the explosive roar of the cannon. Not the sound of the firing pin hammering home, nor the echo of the spent shells falling against the ground. Not the screams of the rats, tightly packed inside the barn in anticipation of their coming ambush, nor the muted shredding of solid shot passing through their flesh. Not even the groans of the barn itself, whose infrastructure was not built to absorb punishment of the kind it was suffering. Barley raked his fire across the building with the cool deliberateness of a professional, as if this was a routine errand, of no particular interest. The rat who had first broken cover spent a moment held upright by the sheer momentum of the tossed lead, jerking maniacally like a marionette, before collapsing into a torn heap of gristle. One of his comrades hidden in the loft inside managed to ring out a rifle shot, but before a second could be managed Barley compensated, sending a spray of metal through the upper story and silencing any further rejoinders.

Then it was over, the gun going still, a great mass of corpses left to rot in the noonday sun, or growing cool in the shade of the now ruined barn.

Gertrude tamped down her pipe. "I suppose they were imagining the same thing."

Barley allowed himself a half-smile. "Buncha daydreamers."

Barley had been right, that day when the Captain came to see him. There was no one who killed like he did.

# Chapter 24

# Best Laid Plans

After thirty seconds or so the artillery ended. The Captain pulled a cigar from his pocket, lit it, and took a few shallow draws. "You sure?"

A knock on the door was followed a moment later by Cinnabar's snout. "Everything all right in here?"

"Fine," the Captain said. "Just having a chat."

Cinnabar nodded, then retreated back into the afternoon sun.

The Captain let the cigar smoke pool around his furred face. "Well?" he asked, after a while.

"Surely you don't expect me to talk?"

"More than expect."

"My rat did too good a job. I'll be dead in five minutes, and if you try cutting at me I'm sure I'll go sooner."

"You've got too thick a hide to be trying torture in any circumstance," the Captain said.

Zapata coughed up something that had more red in it than yellow. "Too kind."

"But you're going to talk to me anyway."

"And why would I do that, Captain? Why would I think to help you?"

"Because you hate Mephetic every bit as much as you hate me. And it'll do you good, heading off into the next world knowing that one of us is going to kill the other, sure as eggs is eggs."

Zapata's laugh shook his torso violently and unquestionably shortened his life. "Maybe you'll both go together," he said, "and I'll watch you walk into hell arm in arm!"

The Captain shrugged. Theology was not his strong point. "Maybe."

"Give me a shot of whiskey."

The Captain got up from his chair, grabbed the jug from off the floor, and laid it beside the soon-to-be corpse. Despite his injury Zapata managed to uncork it and raise it to his lips. Liquor spilled out his belly, along with blood.

"They've got him on a train circling around Santa Theresa, back and forth through no-man's-land. Had him there ever since they gave him shelter back in aught-six. My people assumed that way the Younger couldn't make an issue of it, but they still had him on hand in case he ever proved useful. Wait around until you see a train that looks like it shouldn't be there. That'll be the one to hit."

"All right," the Captain said simply, standing.

"You're a real son of a bitch, you know that?" Zapata said, taking a final drink. "I think maybe I hope Mephetic gets you after all."

The Captain didn't wait to watch him die, didn't pay him another thought, just opened the door and walked smoothly into the light.

## Chapter 25

# That Evening . . .

They were sitting around the fire when Elf came scuttling into view, awkward gait made more so by the corpse she held in one talon. The assembled party, expecting her arrival, managed to react with less shock than at her first appearance, though with no greater warmth. Most of them had hoped she would catch a bullet at some point during the day's events.

Hoped, but not expected. It didn't do to bet against the Elf.

She shuffled her way into the light, her one functioning wing speeding her ascent up the hill. When she reached the apex she dropped the dead rat against the sand and began to preen.

"Howdy, Elf," the Captain said after a long moment.

Elf's sharp beak darted up from her feathers, and she stared at the Captain as if just then recognizing him. "Hello, Captain." Her pupils, ebony pearls offset in yellow, swiveled across the unfriendly row of faces. "Hello, friends."

Cordiality dispensed with, Elf went back to cleaning herself.

The Captain broke the silence a second time. "Elf."

"Yes, Captain?"

"What's with the corpse?"

Elf looked down at her feet and bobbled her head in a sort of half-nod. "Oh. Yes. He was trying to escape. There was another one, but I decided not to bring it."

"What possessed you to bring this one?" Bonsoir piped up.

Elf didn't respond, though after another moment she looked back up and asked, "Did you receive satisfactory answers?"

The Captain nodded. "We're off to Santa Theresa in the morning."

"Well and good. I think I'll take the evening air, before slumber calls me to her bosom."

No one said anything for a while. Then the Captain said, "You go ahead and do that."

After she had disappeared from the firelight, though likely well before she had left earshot, Bonsoir snorted from his perch. "If I carried every corpse I ever made, I'd be one myself from the weight."

"Get rid of it," the Captain said, turning back to his drink.

Bonsoir thought about grumbling, but it didn't do to argue with the Captain. He carried the dead rat a few dozen yards beyond their campsite. They'd be gone before it started to rot.

## Chapter 26

# With Less Liquor Than Earlier . . .

"Coulda been the Dragon," Barley said. It was him and Boudica and the stoat, and they were drinking quietly a little way out of the firelight.

"Wasn't the Dragon," Boudica answered with some degree of certainty.

"Why not? I know he goes back a ways with the Captain, but then . . ."

"What do you remember about that day?"

"What's there to remember?" Bonsoir asked. "We'd won, or almost. Just a bit of cleanup left, then it was a long retirement, rolls of gold coin and fetching females. We were in the main room of the keep, drinking like we did every night, and then—"

"And then our old friends started killing us," Barley cut in, and you might almost have believed him bitter about it.

"Where were you when that started to happen?" Boudica asked.

"Leaking liquor," Barley said.

Bonsoir shrugged. "Underneath a table, I suppose. I was so drunk I can barely remember."

"If you'd been there"—Boudica pointed at Barley—"and if you'd been sober"—she shifted her finger over to the stoat—"you wouldn't need to ask."

"But I was drunk," Bonsoir responded, "so you'll have to tell me."

Boudica cocked her head back at the fire, and at the salamander quietly sitting there. "You ever notice, however much he drinks, he never gets drunk? When they came through the door he was the only one sober enough to do anything about it. Put down Alphonze the hedgehog, both of the Squirrel twins. Put them down like they was nothing. If it wasn't for the Dragon, the Captain would be dead, and I'd be dead, and you'd probably be dead too."

They chewed that over for a while. Then Bonsoir spat it back out. "That proves nothing. The cold-bloods, they aren't like us. They kill just for the fun of it."

"You kill for fun," Barley responded.

"Not like he does."

"Wasn't Cinnabar," Boudica said again, though this time she seemed less certain.

## Chapter 27

# With the Jugs Half-Empty . . .

Barley and Bonsoir were standing a ways out from the main campsite, pissing with the wind.

"I'm pretty sure it wasn't me," Bonsoir said.

Barley laughed, but he wasn't.

## Chapter 28

# As the Stocks Grew Low . . .

"I figure it wasn't the Captain," Boudica said. "And if it was Gertrude we'd all be dead."

"Coulda been Elf," Bonsoir said.

"It wasn't Elf."

"No," Bonsoir agreed. "It wasn't Elf."

# Chapter 29

# At the Bottom of the Kegs . . .

"You sure it wasn't Boudica?" Bonsoir began.

"Not really," Barley said.

"I know who it was." Neither Bonsoir nor Barley had any idea the owl was there in the moment before she spoke, so perfectly did her feathers blend in with the night, and so utterly silent were her movements. Elf raked them back and forth with eyes that were like talons. "I do," she said, before hobbling back off into the darkness.

Bonsoir turned back to the badger. "I believe her."

"Me too."

# Chapter 30

# A Smoke Before Sleep

It was just the two of them, as it often was lately, as it had been in the past. The fire had burned down to its embers, and the night had overtaken everything. Cinnabar lit a cigarette and handed it off to Gertrude, then started rolling another. "Were you surprised?"

"When they betrayed us?"

"Yes."

"I was."

"That surprises me."

"No one is as smart as they think I am. No one is as anything as they think anyone is."

"No, I suppose they aren't."

"Except you. You're exactly as fast as they say."

A match sparked. Two dots of light bobbed in the dark. "Why did they do it?" Cinnabar asked.

"Why do you think they did it?"

"I'm not as smart as you."

"Still."

"The usual reasons," Cinnabar suggested. "Greed, lust, revenge, power, boredom. The Captain is unlovable."

The one light was all by its lonesome. "Yes."

"If they'd bothered to ask me—"

"Let's not go down that road."

"No. I was surprised at the Quaker, though. If ever two things loved each other . . ."

"What is love against instinct? We're all animals, after all. How long can a thing go against its nature?"

It was completely dark. "And what is our nature?"

But the question was too obvious to need an answer.

# Chapter 31

# An Expected Reversal

Mephetic did not get angry when word came that Zapata had failed. He had figured Zapata would fail. The armadillo was loud, and the armadillo was hard, and the armadillo was even mean, so far as that went. But the armadillo was no match for the Captain. Still, it had been worth a try. Even the toughest bastard can catch a bullet in the back of the spine.

He had tripped up the last time, hadn't he? Five years they'd gone back and forth, tearing apart the kingdom during the War of Two Brothers. An inaccurate name, one he wouldn't have chosen. The Toads, Elder and Younger, had taken no part in the conflict—hell, Mephetic's pawn had been trashed on opium so much of the time he couldn't tell his head from his trunk. Really it had always been between him and the Captain, half a decade of red hands and black deeds. And the Captain would have come out the better of it, if Mephetic hadn't managed to turn half his company and even one in his inner circle. Many were the Captain's virtues—if being a bloodthirsty, iron-hearted, grim-eyed bastard can be considered laudatory—but he wasn't an easy animal to work for, and there had been plenty happy to do him wrong, especially with the promise of gold waiting at the end of their betrayal. In the event, the Captain had ended up killing most of them, so Mephetic hadn't even had to pay.

Not that Mephetic doubted his own forces would be any slower to knife his back, should the circumstances call for it, or even allow. They were deep in the heart of the inner keep, and Puss and Brontë were playing a game of pinochle. It seemed as though Puss was winning, though both participants were cheating so egregiously it was hard to say for certain.

Mephetic took the missive he'd been reading and tossed it into the fire.

"I take it they escaped your little trap?" Puss asked. Puss rarely missed the chance to revel in the misfortune of another, though the Captain's survival little benefited him either.

"This one."

"They must be awful tough"—Puss paused a moment to lick down a piece of fur—"if they managed to put the armadillo in the ground."

"I doubt they bothered to bury him."

"What about this Dragon?" Brontë asked, slipping a card surreptitiously, or what she imagined to be surreptitiously, from the fold of her dress. "Is he as fast as they say?"

"He's fast."

"How fast?"

"Slower than a bolt of lightning. Somewhat quicker than a hummingbird's wing."

Puss laughed. Brontë realized she'd just been made fun of, thought about getting angry, then remembered who Mephetic was and laughed also. There were upsides to being the boss, Mephetic often thought. It had been worth it, all the blood he'd needed to spill to get here. Wasn't his blood, anyway.

"And my bird?" the Quaker interrupted, the words stretched across the thing's forked tongue. "What about my bird? What about my sweet, lost bird?"

Puss stopped laughing. Brontë had already stopped laughing, but she looked a bit less jovial all the same.

"She's there," Mephetic said, making sure not to look away.

"You're sure?"

"Our spy says so."

The Quaker tucked his head back into his coils, but didn't say anything else. He seemed happy, to the degree that such a quality could be attributed to a rattlesnake.

"Far be it for me to play spoiler"—though in fact there was nothing Puss enjoyed more—"but I can't help but observe that, thus far, the Captain's hardly playing according to plan."

"Zapata wasn't my plan. I've got a man on the inside."

"The one who betrayed them the last time? If this . . . mouse"—the last word spat out with the sort of contempt one would expect from an ancestral predator—"is all you say, I'd be wary of relying on the same gag twice."

"It's not the same gag. And it's not the same traitor."

# PART THE THIRD

# Chapter 32

# The Soul of a Shrew

The conductor was the sort of shrew who took his job very seriously. He had joined the company as a pup, just after the last track was laid. He been first in line at the office in fact, hat in hand, hopeful, desperate even, for employment. Not as an engineer, of course, nor as one of the brutes shoveling coal. It was not the trains that interested him really; their whistles were too noisy and their smokestacks too dirty. Rather, it was something about the idea of the railroad itself—a steel web crisscrossing the territories, strangling the land, operating according to principles of mathematical purity unseen in any organic creature—that fired his imagination, that gave him a secret and delicious thrill. The conductor was the sort of creature whose wildest fantasies were filled with ledgers that balanced perfectly, and rows of clocks chiming in eternal unison.

He had signed on as a ticket-taker, a private soldier in that small army of creatures whose function was to mark paper and look at the marks on paper and mark the paper again, and sometimes, if the marks were not right, to look up from the paper and squint their bespectacled eyes (spectacles were virtually a professional requirement) and say, "Sorry, sir, but it seems your luggage was sent to Poughkeepsie and not Kalamazoo. You will receive it within eight to seventy-five business days, a business day being defined as Tuesdays and alternate Thursdays." This last was the part the shrew liked the most.

He had fulfilled his duties faithfully, moving up the ranks from junior assistant ticket-taker to assistant ticket-taker to ticket-taker to conductor. He was never sick and never late for work. He never took time off for personal reasons, never visited an ill relative or attended a friend's nuptials. Two years earlier, in reward for this diligent service, he had been assigned to the Antelope Limited. "A critical posting," his supervisor had informed him, "a sign of our trust in your sagacity, your prudence, and, most importantly," he had said, raising his eyes archly, "your discretion."

In the years since the conductor had wondered, occasionally, why there was a massive metal door dividing the front carriage from the rest of the train, and also who lived inside said carriage, and why their presence necessitated armed guards, and finally, whether those guards were meant to ensure the safety of this precious cargo or make sure that it never left. But the conductor didn't wonder much. Wondering wasn't his job, after all. Whatever was going on in the front carriage, it gave him the right, in his own mind at least, to be twice as carping and cantankerous as he might otherwise have been, to scan every rider with thorough, even exaggerated, scrutiny.

Though even under normal circumstances he wouldn't have allowed them on the train. Maybe the badger. Despite his size he seemed good-humored, with an open face and a generous smile. And the opossum, she looked harmless enough, lazy and slow as sweet molasses.

But not the salamander. The conductor didn't like cold-bloods as a rule, and there was something about this burnt-red specimen that was particularly off-putting. No, not the salamander, and certainly not the mouse, with his nasty scar and his eye that stared at the conductor as if waiting to repay an injury.

The conductor was making his rounds before the train left the station, checking on the functionaries beneath him, ensuring that they were just the right amount of peevish, unhelpful without being aggressive. When he entered the car and saw those two sitting together, the salamander and the mouse, he made a mental note to find something wrong with their papers, or their luggage—to detect or invent a reason why it was that they needed to miss this particular train. He would be very apologetic about it, of course; he would blame it on regulations and his own superiors, sympathize with them in their misfortune, but march them back onto the platform all the same.

With this serious but secretly enjoyable task ahead of him, the conductor was waylaid by the sudden chirrup of a nearby mole. "Excuse me, sir. Excuse me!" The second time she yelled loudly, though the conductor had already been stopping. "Sir, I require your assistance, please!"

The conductor bristled. The conductor did not like being interrupted in the course of his duties, and he did not like being yelled at. He didn't like a lot of things, truth be told. Still, a customer was a customer, and the conductor was nothing if not professional. "Of course, ma'am," he began, his voice exactly how you would expect. "How can I help you?"

"Finally." Behind her bifocals the mole's eyes were huge and blind and stupid. "I asked the muskrat who was selling the tickets, and he said that he didn't know but that you might know, and so that's why I'm asking you. Do you know?"

"Know what?"

"Where my bags are, obviously."

"I'm afraid, ma'am, that I don't have any—"

"Of course you haven't, I wouldn't expect you have, but surely you must know someone who *has*, mustn't you? When one gets on a train in the Capital one expects to find one's bags when one gets to Last Gulch, doesn't one? Assuming one is getting off in Last Gulch, which was where I changed trains."

"Of course, but—"

"You certainly can't expect me to survive forever with just the dress I'm wearing, can you? What do you take me for? A church mouse?"

"No, obviously not—"

"Good. I'm glad to see we can agree to that much. So what exactly do you plan to do about it?"

"About what?"

"My bags not being on this train," said the mole, as if one of them were an idiot.

"If you would just excuse me for a moment, I promise to come help you just as soon as—"

But then the whistle blew, and the great iron steed bucked forward, and the conductor knew he had lost. For all that he might have wished otherwise, he could not very well throw a passenger off a moving train just because he didn't like the look of him. He turned his attention back to the shrill mole, and her problem about which he could do nothing.

## Chapter 33

# Just Past Ciudad del Gato . . .

The badger got up from where he was sitting and ambled forward, squeezing his bulk through the narrow rows of seats. The conductor saw him from a carriage away, and his stomach dropped out from under him, because there was absolutely no way a creature of such size could fit in the bathroom. He excused himself from explaining to another passenger—an elderly turtle, he thought she was elderly at least, it was hard to tell with turtles—why it wasn't possible for her to use her unassigned ticket anytime today, or anytime tomorrow, or really, just any time at all, and he approached the badger, trying to come up with a polite way of informing him that he was going to have to hold his bladder for the better part of three hours.

It was only then that he noticed the mouse, the one he hadn't liked, walking in the long shadow cast by the badger, and behind him the salamander whom he had liked even less. The conductor—who was not a particularly clever sort of creature, but who wasn't quite dumb as a carpenter's nail—began to think that today might turn out to be one of those days where things failed to abide by their proper routine. The conductor hated those sorts of days.

The conductor turned around and headed forward until he came to the first-class compartments. A chubby vole sat as guardian between the two sections, making sure the hoi polloi didn't get any ideas above their station. His name was Harold, and the most important thing he had learned in his life, as far as he was concerned, was that it was entirely possible to sleep with one's eyes open, or at least open enough to deceive passersby, if one was willing to put in a bit of practice. True, it wasn't as good as a full-on nap, but any degree of slumber was better than waking. As far as Harold was concerned, the better part of existence lay in those little moments of oblivion that preceded the last.

The conductor hustled past without realizing his protector was dim to the world; he even took some degree of comfort in the barrier he imagined he was putting between himself and the badger. Indeed, as soon as he reached the first-class compartment, with its slightly more comfortable seats and vaguely polished décor, he felt a concrete sense of relief. Nothing bad, after all, ever happened to the rich.

Sad to say, his optimism was short-lived. Through the

glass door separating the two carriages the conductor saw the badger continue forward, Harold forced awake by his heavy footfalls, coming up from his seat to say something. And then Harold was back in his seat and in a deeper slumber than he had theretofore been enjoying, courtesy of the badger's backhand.

At that moment the conductor did the bravest thing he had ever done in his life, which was to run screaming toward the front of the train. When he reached the guarded carriage he banged on the door until the peephole slid open. The conductor did not know the rat inside—the conductor had never before tried to enter the front carriage, had never even acknowledged its existence. That was against the rules, and the conductor, in case you had somehow missed the point by now, was the sort of creature who liked following them.

"They're coming!" he yelled.

"Who?"

The conductor moved aside swiftly, allowing the rat to get a view of the troupe of creatures following in his wake. The conductor himself did not bother to turn around, and to judge by the sudden doubling of the circumference of the rat's eyes, it was just as well that he did not.

The door flew open. The conductor bolted through. The door slammed shut.

The conductor had hoped that inside would be a dozen soldiers in full battle gear, or maybe a couple of hedgehogs with heavy artillery. So fear followed closely upon the heels of disappointment when he discovered that the impregnable fortress attached to the front of his train was crewed by two rats who looked barely out of their litter, holding their rifles gingerly and giving off a very distinct smell of terror.

"What do we do now?" one of them asked. The other rat, the rat who had been looking through the peephole and had seen the badger, didn't say anything.

Needless to say, this was not the reaction that the shrew had anticipated. But he surprised himself, as he had several times so far that day, with his sangfroid, with his mental fortitude, with his keen sense of battlefield tactics. "We keep the door shut," he answered.

The rats nodded in unison. The conductor could hear the rumbling of the badger and his companions from the other carriage and tensed himself for the inevitable blows—blows that did not come.

Gathering up his nerve, the conductor opened the peephole and looked out. Behind the door he could see the opossum and the badger standing around, neither looking particularly agitated. "This is double-reinforced steel!" yelled the conductor, trying to cover his fear. "You'll never break it down!"

The Badger scratched at the thick fur of his head awhile before answering. "Yeah, you're probably right."

"I am?"

It was then that the conductor felt air blowing in through an open window, which gave him a brief moment of happiness, because it was a hot day after all, and the wind cool, but this was followed quickly by a much more potent sense of despair.

"Keep the door shut," said a thickly accented voice from behind him. "That is a fine plan. That is the sort of plan a fellow ought to be proud to have come up with."

# Chapter 34

# The Loot

Bonsoir opened the reinforced-steel door and the Captain came through an instant later, stepping over the corpses with unstudied disinterest. A partition had been erected two-thirds of the way down the compartment, and the mouse stopped at the entrance to it, nodding at Cinnabar behind him. The Dragon slid the gate sideways with his usual extraordinary celerity, and before it banged against the frame he had both revolvers out, ready for whatever was waiting for them.

A moment passed. Cinnabar holstered his guns.

Bonsoir came in behind him, rolling a cigarette. "This is an unfortunate surprise," he said, slipping his tobacco pouch underneath his beret before lighting his smoke with a match struck off his boot.

"I guess this changes things," Cinnabar said.

The Captain reached over and plucked the cigarette from Bonsoir's mouth. He took a long, slow drag before responding. "No, it doesn't," he said. Then he handed the smoke to Cinnabar and nodded at Bonsoir. "Tell Barley to grab him. We've got a long hike back to town." He turned and walked back down the carriageway.

Cinnabar and Bonsoir exchanged a look. The stoat shrugged and went off to find Barley. The Captain had spoken, and the Captain's was the final word.

# Chapter 35

# A Question of Numbers

Mephetic had spent a long time considering the number of rats he should bring. Too many and the Captain might sniff them out and bolt—the Captain was the cagiest creature Mephetic had ever dealt with, cagier than any weasel, polecat, or fox. Too few, of course, and the Captain's crew would gun their way out, because as cagey as the Captain was, he was every bit as tough, and the animals he'd assembled were even tougher. Mephetic had decided to err on too many—at least that way he didn't run the risk of ending up a corpse. The Captain wasn't the only cagey thing living in the Gardens.

So it was Mephetic and Puss and Brontë and two full companies of the rat guard, a hundred grim-faced rodents carrying heavy iron, hiding low in the hills around the bar. The Quaker was slithering about, where exactly Mephetic wasn't sure. You didn't really order the Quaker to do anything, you just pointed him in a direction and held your breath.

Mephetic was down on his stomach, scanning the front road with his spyglass. Puss and Brontë were beside him, for once equally silent. In the final few moments before evening fell completely, Mephetic caught the first glimpse of the companions coming up over the hill. He held his breath in anticipation, hoping he hadn't over-played his hand.

And indeed, there was a moment when he thought for sure he had mucked it. The six of them were tramping toward the bar when the Captain, standing in the middle of the pack, perked his nose up suddenly, sniffing at the air. Mephetic cursed beneath his breath and readied the order to rush them en masse, knowing it wouldn't work, knowing he'd lose half his rats trying. Still, there were al-ways more rats—fecundity was one of the few virtues of the species.

But then the Captain swung his head back down, tipped his hat over it, and kept on moving. A few minutes afterward, all six of the companions were comfortably en-sconced inside. They'd come straight back after hitting the train, and they looked dusty and tired. They'd lay their burdens on the ground and start hitting the liquor, and after they'd done that awhile, Mephetic would hit them back.

"What are we waiting for?" Puss asked. Puss wore a satin vest and matching pants. They had begun the day white, though having spent the better part of an hour pressed against the sand they could no longer claim that distinction. He had a pair of pearl-handled pistols hanging at his waist. He looked like a rodeo clown, but that didn't make him any less dangerous.

"You're waiting for me to give the signal," Mephetic snapped. "Because I'm the boss, and no one does anything without me telling them to do it."

Puss looked at Mephetic awhile, and then he looked at the ground. Mephetic decided at that moment that if Puss survived this go-round with the Captain he would make sure the cat didn't survive much longer. Puss was getting to be more trouble than he was worth. Probably that would also necessitate doing away with Brontë, who had some vague notion that she and the cat were friends—insofar as two violent, amoral sociopaths were capable of that sort of connection—but that was fine. The Gardens would hardly be a worse place with them propping up tulips.

But first thing was first, and first was the Captain. Some twenty minutes after the companions had headed through the front door the traitor came hobbling out back, lit a cigarette, gave a little wave, and walked back inside.

"Send the rats in first," Mephetic said. "Unless you feel like martyring yourself in service of the Toad."

To judge by the space Brontë and Puss put between themselves and the company of soldiers, this honor held little interest. They moved carefully, slowly, a mass of crawling creatures working their way through the underbrush, a tightening noose of grim-faced rodents. When they reached the tavern a dozen of them clambered stealthily up to the roof, while their comrades fanned out around the building. Revolvers were cocked. Rifles were aimed. Death hung thick.

The first rat kicked down the door and went barreling inside, came out again almost as quick, stumbling off the porch and into the dust. The rest proved slower to make their ingress, though with a few shouted words from Brontë they managed it, firing blindly inside, as if the companions were fool enough to sprint into the face of their guns.

Mephetic knew otherwise, of course, and he shifted his glasses to the front, waiting for their inevitable attempt at a breakout. It wasn't long coming. The Dragon went first, pistols firing; rats falling like flies, dropping from the rooftop, dying gut-shot in the dust. Mephetic realized his entire body was tense with excitement; he was almost ready to vomit from the sheer adrenaline coursing through his veins. And moreover, he realized he wasn't sure which side he was rooting for, or at least his heart thrilled at each sudden new bit of brilliance on the part of the companions. When the badger (what was his name again? Oat? Millet? It didn't matter, particularly; he wouldn't be around much longer) took a rifle bullet in the shoulder and kept coming, grabbing the rat who had hit him by one hand and swinging him like a lash into another, the *crack* of bone audible even from his distant perch, Mephetic let out a cheer loud enough to draw the attention of his bodyguard, though of course they were wise enough to pretend they hadn't noticed.

Cinnabar and the opossum were in front, and though the latter generally did her business with a long rifle, she had no problem putting down rats up close, her revolver doing sedate but mortal work. Of course it was nothing like the Dragon, who seemed like his namesake to all but breathe death, the only check on his violence the need to reload. So constant was this torrent of lead that the pack of rats, the army of rats, the endless wave of rats, scurried backward for the safety of the bar, for any plank of wood or bit of stone or shallow indentation in the sand that might give them cover from the killing metal.

It occurred to Mephetic belatedly that he had underestimated the Captain; he had forgotten in the long years since they'd last seen each other just how dangerous the mouse was. He should have brought another company of soldiers; he ought to have drained the Kingdom of killers; he ought to have hired mercenaries and impressed citizens, if he'd wanted to make certain the Captain and his companions wouldn't walk away.

Or he could have just done what he did, which was turn one of the Captain's creatures against him. The Captain might have figured on Reconquista; it was his second turn at betrayal, after all. But there was no way the Captain could have known Gertrude was—well, a mole. They were taking up the rear, the Captain's scattergun roaring back into the bar, the Captain roaring just as loud, his one eye as dead as the other, when Gertrude reached up behind him and did something—Mephetic couldn't make it out distinctly, but whatever it was, it dropped the Captain to the ground.

The rats swarmed then, so fast and so many that they seemed almost like a single creature, or some impersonal force, a rain cloud or a wave beating against the shore. There was a moment when it seemed as if the companions might try to save him, but it didn't last long. There was nothing to do but beat an escape—at least that was what they ended up doing, laying down covering fire and disappearing down the road. The surviving rats made an attempt to continue after them, but really it wasn't altogether serious, and with half their number lying dead on the ground, you couldn't very well blame them.

But that was fine—the companions were dangerous like a loaded gun: harmless without someone to pull the trigger. They'd go back to whatever they had been doing before the mouse forced them out of retirement, and they'd leave Mephetic free to continue running the Gardens as he had before. This thought gave Mephetic a quick splash of sadness—back to the endless bureaucratic drudgery, the routine the Captain's return had broken him out of—but of course there was nothing to be done about it.

Puss carried the Captain, still unconscious from whatever the mole had done to him, back up the hill and left him lying in the dust. The rats had stripped him of his weapons, and they hadn't been kind in doing so. Mephetic waited patiently until the Captain awoke, and his good eye struggled its way open. Mephetic wanted to make sure he was the first thing the Captain saw, as indeed he was.

"Hello again, Captain," Mephetic said, smiling. "It's been a long time."

# PART THE FOURTH

# Chapter 36

# An Awful End

After he had finished betraying the Captain, and the skunk and his forces had dumped their numerous dead in an open trough and headed back to the Capital, Reconquista locked the door and hung a CLOSED sign over it. The sign would never come down. Reconquista hadn't liked operating a bar, had only done so after he'd blown through most of the coin he'd gotten from Mephetic the first time he'd betrayed the Captain. But he'd be more careful with this round. He would migrate to the Kingdom to the South, where his money would spend further. Get a hacienda and some broken-down peasants to work it, bring in a few fat-bottomed dams to while away his last days. He didn't have so many left, he knew.

*Click, click, click.*

Reconquista had started drinking just after he'd put up the sign, drinking and drinking with a purpose. It was, to be very clear, not out of any sense of guilt. Reconquista had never felt anything toward the Captain, nor toward any of the gang, nor toward anyone else, truth be told. And after all, it was the Captain's fault that he only had half a body, the Captain's fault for shooting Alfalfa the hare while Alfalfa the hare had been holding a stick of dynamite and standing next to Reconquista. Of course it had been Reconquista who had convinced Alfalfa to light that stick and to try to kill the Captain with it, Alfalfa and the Quaker and some of the others, now all dead—but then Reconquista did not count any particular sense of fairness among his virtues.

*Click, click, click.*

He was surprised that Gertrude had turned traitor; he could admit that. He hadn't known that was coming, hadn't bothered to try to turn the mole five years back, hadn't tried with the mole or any of the other inner circle. He'd figured them for saps, thick with those strange notions of loyalty that led animals into the grave at some earlier date than was strictly necessary. And also, being higher up in the Captain's ranks they were in for a larger cut of the spoils, had less incentive for betrayal.

*Click, click, click.*

Reconquista, by contrast, had known he wouldn't be getting a very significant slice—oh, the rest of the boys were friendly enough to him, in their backhanded way, but he wasn't tough, not tough like Barley or the Dragon, and the fact that he'd been with the Captain since the beginning, or nearly since, wouldn't have guaranteed him any more than crumbs. And what was the point of the whole thing, if it hadn't been to make out like bandits in the end? Certainly he had no loyalty to the Elder, none of them did. It was pure self-interest for everyone; he'd just been sharp enough to make good.

*Click, click, click.*

No, it wasn't guilt. If Reconquista had to take a guess why he was drinking himself into a coma, it would have been because he knew he was getting old. This was his last scrap—he would never again get to feel adrenaline pumping through his veins, never again stand above the corpse of an enemy, or an ally for that matter. He would while away his few remaining years a farting, toothless, one-armed geezer.

*Click, click, click.*

It was enough to make Reconquista want to take another drink of whiskey. And why not? Who was left to stop him, after all?

*Click, click, click.*

Reconquista got up from his seat, wooden leg struggling to find purchase. He made his way behind the bar, got the sawed-off shotgun he kept for protection. It had a hell of a kick, especially with Reconquista only having the one hand, but the spread made accuracy less than critical. All you needed to do was aim in the general direction of whatever you wanted dead, pull the trigger, and dig a hole. It was this last part that Reconquista cared for least.

*Click, click, click.*

With his one good hand he held the butt, sliding his hook beneath the barrel. Then he stumbled out to the back porch. He was too drunk to be fearful, and anyway there wasn't any reason to be. The Captain was captured, soon to be dead, the companions scattered or turned traitor themselves.

*Click, click, click.*

He had been sure it was coming from the back, but standing on the porch now he couldn't see anything beyond the outhouse and the scrub brush that led into the desert.

*Click, click, click.*

The shadows were getting long, and Reconquista was getting frightened, frightened through the bottle of whiskey in his stomach, frightened down into his bones and into the bones of his absent arm and his absent leg. "Who's out here?" he asked stupidly, knowing it was stupid as he was asking it.

*Click, click, click.*

"I'm warning you!" he yelled, which was an even stupider thing to say, because whatever was waiting for him didn't need to be fearful, and knew it.

The shadows descended, and though he had time to fire off two full barrels of double aught they didn't do any good, flew harmlessly into the sky and then dropped harmlessly onto the ground. The shadow covered him and then the shadow was Elf, and then Elf's beak and Elf's claws began to do what beaks and claws do, and Reconquista screamed.

The rat's death was quick, but terrible all the same.

# Chapter 37

# A New Cellmate

There was only one creature in the dungeons when they brought the Captain in: a squirrel, though he was so thick with dirt and bent with age it took a moment to be sure. An empty prison is generally a sign of a well-run state, of a happy populace with no need to engage in crime. In this particular instance it was a sign of the opposite, of a nation that had declared anything worse than shoplifting a capital offense and was quick to execute that policy, and, for that matter, its citizens. Which is to say that a great many creatures went into Mephetic's dungeons, but they didn't stay long, a way station on the path to the dirt.

That the squirrel had remained alive so long was a clerical error, though whether of a benign or malignant sort, it was hard to say. He had gone mad quite quickly, the rambunctious energy of his species forced inward by the constraints of his cell. He could no longer remember what his crime had been, or what he had done before his time there, or what his name was, or what the sun looked like.

The guards dumped the Captain into his cell, made promises to see him again soon, and left. The Captain stood, brushed himself off, and scowled. He reached for his purse of tobacco, realized it had been taken, and scowled some more. It had been two days since his capture, the result of Gertrude's treachery and Mephetic's cleverness, and the forty-eight hours had been less than pleasant. If the situation were reversed, Mephetic wouldn't have lasted that long. The Captain would have put him in the ground as soon as he had him; double-tap and then food for the ants. The Captain didn't torture except when he had to, and he never, ever, left an enemy alive.

Mephetic, it seemed, was crueler. Or more foolish.

"Tell me a story," the squirrel chittered all of a sudden, climbing up the bars of the cell, his tail flaring back and forth, caked with muck and grime and other, nastier things. "Tell me a story," he repeated, louder this time. "Tell me a story or I'll carve out your eyes, tell me a story or I'll chew out your tongue, tell me a story or I'll sneak into your cell and make your bones into jelly!"

He was screaming at this point, though the Captain seemed not to notice, staring hard at the concrete walls.

The squirrel dropped down to the floor. "Tell me a story," he said, "or I'll cry."

Pity was generally no more a motivator of the Captain than fear—but for whatever reason he started to speak then. "Once there were two brothers."

The squirrel crossed his legs and rested his head on his hand, eager as a prized student, his tail like a faded hairbrush held upright.

"The two brothers were the heirs to a great kingdom. A kingdom prosperous and happy, a kingdom that, split between them, was still more than any animal would ever need or want."

From somewhere far off, there was a sound.

"But for the two brothers half of everything wasn't nearly enough, and so they began to plot and to scheme against each other, and finally, in time, turned to open battle."

The sound grew louder, though not yet distinct. It was an unfriendly sound, this much could be said with certainty.

"Since the brothers were as cowardly as they were rapacious, and no sort of soldiers, they hired animals who would fight for them—cruel, strong, dangerous—and they let them loose upon their kingdom. And war raged between the two brothers, across the length and breadth of their lands—until finally, the leader of the forces of the elder brother, being crueler, and stronger, and more dangerous, proved victorious."

The sound was prolonged, vigorous. The squirrel didn't seem to notice, however, so engrossed was he in the Captain's story. The Captain probably noticed, but the Captain had heard enough screaming not to get excited about hearing more. He started to talk louder himself, louder and more rapidly, either to drown out the sound or simply from the furor of the narrative.

"But the elder brother and his forces had traitors in their midst, and they betrayed their comrades in their moment of triumph, breaking their power and bringing the younger brother to the throne. And the armies of the elder brother were scattered across the kingdom and beyond, and most thought them dead and buried, and forgot them."

More screams, and gunfire, and something louder than gunfire—dynamite, maybe?

"But they weren't dead, only battered, and they nourished hatred in their hearts, fed off of it, let it warm them in the cold, began to love their hatred as the only thing left to them. And as the kingdom's fortunes faded, and as the land descended into tyranny and poverty, the armies of the elder brother saw their moment."

The door to the jail flew open, burst right off its hinges, Barley coming in smooth behind it. His shoulder was bandaged but he carried his organ-gun without any trouble. Cinnabar slipped in an instant afterward, already reloading his pistols.

"What the hell took you so long?" the Captain asked.

Barley set his cannon on the ground for a moment. "Nice to see you too, Captain." He put his hands around two of the bars, and tensed his shoulders, and then there was a gap wide enough for the Captain to walk through.

Which the Captain did.

"Wait!" the Squirrel screamed. "Wait!"

The Captain turned back to him.

"How does it end?"

The Captain widened his lips around his teeth. Some would call that a smile. They would be wrong. "In blood."

# Chapter 38

# Anticipation (1)

A half-mile out from the inner keep, hanging by her tail in the branches of a tall elm tree, unnoticeable in the darkness, Boudica waited.

# Chapter 39

# A Friendly Smile

Mephetic had told the lieutenant not to lose sight of the mole, not for one second, not even after they'd dropped the mouse off at the dungeons.

The lieutenant hadn't seen what the big deal was. The mole was a typical female of her species, dress strained by wallowing fat, all but blind in any sort of light, and those bifocals might be fetching but they weren't helping her see any better. Even by the standards of a creature that lived underground and ate grubs, Gertrude didn't seem like much to worry about. She had such a friendly smile, after all.

Still, it wasn't the lieutenant's job to second-guess Mephetic. Gertrude was searched very thoroughly at the gatehouse, two rats relieving her of the pistol in her sleeve and the small knife that was nearly unnoticeable at the top of her boot, and even of a pen case they thought might be used as club. Gertrude suffered the indignity without breaking her smile, the absurdity of their caution obvious to all involved. Afterward they laughed and shook hands, except the lieutenant, who kept a firm eye on Gertrude, and a firm scowl on her as well. Before entering the main building the lieutenant turned back to wave to the guards, but they didn't see him or were too lazy to answer, and remained on their stools. Faintly annoyed, he continued in behind Gertrude.

The keep was the biggest and largest and most solid structure in the Capital, in the Gardens, and in any of the neighboring kingdoms. The first walls were massive and imposing, huge slabs of stone that could withstand an artillery shell from close range and not quiver. Inside was a second citadel, the inner keep, small only by the standards of the structure that surrounded it. You'd need an army ten times the size of what Mephetic possessed to besiege it successfully, and even then you'd still need to starve out the garrison. The lieutenant led Gertrude deeper into the castle, past checkpoint after checkpoint of fierce rat guards. At every interval they were stopped to make sure the lieutenant was who he said he was, that the prisoner hadn't pulled a fast one or somehow subverted her captor. At every interval the mole was respectful, amiable even, laughing and glad-handing with the rat guards. Still, the lieutenant didn't let his guard down. There must be something about this mole, if Mephetic had been so worried about her.

They came finally to the boss's office, the nerve center for the whole kingdom. In four years, the lieutenant had never seen the Toad himself—the Lord, he meant, the Lord, you'd catch hell if you forgot that one. Mephetic liked to keep up the pretense, though even the blind beggars in the slums knew the Younger wasn't running anything.

"You've done a fine job, Lieutenant," Gertrude said, as they waited for the door to open. "Mephetic will surely look kindly on you for overseeing something of this importance." The mole leaned in and settled one hand on his wrist, as if to assure him. "You'll make captain by next year—and think how proud your litter will be!"

The lieutenant thanked Gertrude and did indeed think about how happy his pups would be to hear of his promotion, and how he might spend the raise on a toy boat for Alus and a new dress for Serah's doll and a spinning top for Tomas Jr. and . . .

Two scowling rats opened the door, nodded at the lieutenant, and gestured warily for the mole to come in. Well, they could hardly be blamed, though if the lieutenant knew Gertrude, and he felt he did, even after just these few moments, it wouldn't be long before she melted their icy demeanor.

The boss's office was the size of a large dining room, heavy oak shelves full of books that the lieutenant had never seen the boss read, not that there was any reason the boss would feel that this was an activity aided by the lieutenant's presence. There was a desk as heavy as a boulder in the center of the room, and after a bit of time—enough to reinforce that the boss was the boss and you were not—Mephetic came in through a back door and stood in front of it. The lieutenant could tell how happy he was by his smile, which was wide and open, and his tail, which was flaring up and down ever so slightly.

"Why the Underground Man?" he asked Gertrude.

"Instead of Underground Woman?"

"Yes."

"Underground Man sounds scarier."

"That's true," Mephetic agreed. "If I'd had any idea that you were the creature behind organized crime in the city, I'd have . . ."

"Killed me?" Gertrude asked, as if she found nothing particularly objectionable about the notion. "I thought you might feel something like that, which is why I made sure you never learned."

The lieutenant waited until he thought no one was looking, then loosened his collar.

"I'm glad, at least, that you had the good sense to contact me early on in this escapade," Mephetic said. "That mouse needs to learn when he's beaten."

"It won't take. You'll have to kill him."

"I think that's something we can arrange."

Was it hot in here? the lieutenant wondered. The day had been blazing, but the evening had cooled down somewhat—or at least that was what he had been thinking on his way in. But now he was sweating buckshot, could feel it mat down his fur.

"Imagine spending all this time obsessed with something as pointless as revenge," Mephetic said. "That was always the problem with the Captain, if you don't mind me saying so. He was too strong a hater."

"I think perhaps there is no creature in the Gardens with such a talent for it," Gertrude answered, "and so you can hardly be surprised that he chooses to exercise his ability. Fish swim, birds fly, the Captain hates."

"Though not for very much longer."

"It would have been easier if you'd let me know you had another creature on the inside."

"I figured for someone of your abilities, it didn't need to be easy."

"No, indeed," the mole said, smiling her fool-false smile. "I quite enjoy the challenge."

The boss said something, but the lieutenant couldn't quite make it out. If he was being honest, the lieutenant would have had to say that, what with how hot it had gotten, he was no longer as interested in the conversation as he had been. The boss repeated whatever he said, though it took a repetition of that repetition before the lieutenant could finally understand it.

"Lieutenant," Mephetic asked, "what the hell is wrong with you?"

"I assume it's the poison I gave him," Gertrude said. "A concoction of my own making—largely painless, though quite fast-acting."

The lieutenant realized he was on the ground and wondered for a moment how he had gotten there. But it was growing dark, and he turned his mind back to his dam, and his pups, and he hoped they wouldn't miss him too terribly.

Mephetic went for the pistol in his belt, but Gertrude moved with a speed that would have been astonishing in any animal, let alone one who had never before shown any more dexterity than what was required to tie her shoes. A long, heavy needle, the same one that had poisoned half the guards Gertrude had come in contact with since being brought into the citadel, sailed through the air and slammed against Mephetic's drawn revolver, sending the weapon spinning off onto the floor.

The two rats still living, a notch slower than Mephetic and any number of notches slower than Gertrude (a notch not being a literal measurement of speed) went for their own weapons then, though of course it was far too late. Gertrude spread her arms wide, as if in supplication or to offer an embrace, and one thin bit of metal flew into one of the rats, and another thin bit of metal flew into the other, and then it was just Mephetic and the Underground Man alive in the room. And probably not both of them for very much longer.

"A double-cross," Mephetic said. It had been a long time since he'd done his own killing, and apart from his lost gun, he had nothing but a wavy-bladed knife, which he drew swiftly.

"I think this would be a triple-cross, actually, though at some point the sums get hard to do without pen and paper." If Gertrude had any other weapons on her person, she made no move for them, her hands clasped together as if in prayer.

Mephetic feinted left and took a swipe at her, but Gertrude didn't so much as quiver at the ruse, and so neatly dodged the attack itself that for a moment Mephetic got the impression he was fighting not a plump, hairy mole, but some creature composed of the very ether itself.

"I've still got the Captain," Mephetic said, trying to land a verbal blow if he couldn't manage a physical one.

"Not for much longer, I should think. On behalf of the Captain, I'd very much like to thank you for offering us ingress into your impregnable abode. *Our* impregnable abode, I should very soon say."

Mephetic roared and tossed his blade at Gertrude, turning end over end, though by the time it reached the space Gertrude had occupied a scant second earlier Gertrude was no longer occupying it.

Which in fact Mephetic had predicted, having belatedly come to recognize the mole's unnatural speed, a speed that was contrary to her species and indeed to her physical makeup. In fact the skunk, though he had misplayed this particular game, misplayed it quite thoroughly indeed, was no dullard. You will find that skunks as a species are quite clever, as well as being relatively fast and hard to kill.

Though of course, this is not what skunks are famous for. Skunks are famous for one thing and one thing only, and this was the emission that, dropping swiftly and swinging his bushy tail around, Mephetic released from his anal glands, a pulse of foulness that crowded thick through the close air.

# Chapter 40

# The Specialist

Bonsoir slipped a claw into the outer door of the citadel, just before it banged shut. He waited a few seconds to make sure Gertrude had taken care of her end, then tailed afterward. Two dead rats testified to the mole's competence, not that Bonsoir had been foolish enough to doubt it. There was a reason everyone feared the Underground Man. Her reputation did not rest on sand.

Nor was Bonsoir's. He picked the lock on the next door and scampered ahead, as confident in the reinforcements as he had been in the advance force. Gertrude had marked the trail—it was Bonsoir's job to bust it wide open.

Though, in truth, it was a task unworthy of an animal of Bonsoir's talent. The mole had left most of the guards she'd passed dead or rapidly dying, purple-faced or with thick trails of blood leaking from their canines, victims of the seemingly endless packets of poison Gertrude carried on her person. All Bonsoir had to do was take care of the stragglers and make sure all the doors were unlocked, and he had trouble with neither. It didn't hurt that he had lived and worked in the palace for years, knew it like the back of his own black-furred hand.

Bonsoir stopped just short of the antechamber leading into what had been the Captain's office some years earlier. Two guards still waited outside; for some reason Gertrude hadn't managed to find a way to kill either of them. The mole is slipping, Bonsoir thought to himself, though he did not really believe it. The first rat had a knife in his throat all of a sudden, collapsing to the ground so swiftly and so quietly that at first his counterpart seemed to think he had fainted, was bent over trying to revive him when another of Bonsoir's daggers opened a hole in his esophagus through which you could see his spine.

Bonsoir made sure to avoid the blood his handiwork had sent splattering onto the wall. He was a professional, after all.

His task completed, Bonsoir slipped off into the surrounding corridors, knives on his belt and dynamite in his pack, anxious to see what mischief his expertise might wreak.

## Chapter 41

# Anticipation (2)

A half-mile out from the inner keep, hanging by her tail in the branches of a tall elm tree, unnoticeable in the darkness, Boudica waited.

## Chapter 42

# For All Things Are Mortal

Bonsoir had taken care of the guards outside the throne room but he hadn't done anything about the door itself. The Captain was a competent lock pick himself, as was Cinnabar, but it was easier just to have Barley break it down, which was what they did, the badger rushing against the door and then rushing right back out again, retching up the eggs he'd eaten for breakfast and the whiskey he'd drunk for lunch. With the door open, Mephetic's emanations came billowing out, and rather than join Barley's example Cinnabar and the Captain retreated back down the corridor. The badger followed as soon as he was able, and they let the stink filter out awhile before returning.

Gertrude had died hard. A full blast of Mephetic's reek and still she had struggled, crawling facedown toward the door, her blood streaking against the marble floor. But she had managed to right herself before expiring, leaning against a wall, slump-shouldered, her face mute with the agony of her final moments. The stench that came off her corpse was uncanny, unbearable though Cinnabar bore it, kneeling down beside her, holding his hat to his chest.

"Rough way to die," Barley said, but this was as far as his sympathies went. He had never liked the Underground Man, particularly, and anyway, none of them were very likely to survive till morning.

"Let's go," the Captain said.

But Cinnabar didn't answer.

"Cinnabar."

"One moment."

"We don't have the time."

Everyone knows, of course, that salamanders are a breed apart. Their blood is cold, their humours bitter; they know neither sympathy nor passion. They take no lovers, only mates, and they don't have friends, only allies, and even then only so long as they're convenient. Everyone knows that. Everyone.

"There's time if I say there's time," Cinnabar said.

The Captain stared at him for a long moment but in the end it seemed he agreed, or at least he did not move onward. Cinnabar looked back down at Gertrude and said nothing further. Somewhere below there was the sound of an explosion and the floor rocked uneasily. Something screamed, and then stopped screaming.

Gertrude's eyes were wide and red veined and despairing. Cinnabar closed them and stood. "All right," he said.

# Chapter 43

# Raison d'Être

Bonsoir was having a grand time.

The Captain had been right, that first night when he had come recruiting. Bonsoir had been wasting his time in dusty border towns, amid rundown bars—and more than his time, he had been wasting his genius.

Everything had a purpose, that was the way Bonsoir saw it. Bees make honey, songbirds trill, pretty females strut down the sidewalk on sunny afternoons and pretend they do not know you are looking at them. The rest of the crew, Barley and Cinnabar and so on, they were kick-down-the-door types, guns-blazing types, die-in-the-spotlight-with-blood-on-their-grin types. Not Bonsoir. Bonsoir scuttled down darkened corridors and brought sleep with him—not even death, death was too strong a word for what he brought, for the silence that descended when he came. That was Bonsoir's purpose, that was why Bonsoir existed. And what is more joyous than to act according to our innermost nature?

Which brings us back to: Bonsoir was having a grand time.

Though it must be said, Bonsoir's mind was not occupied solely with pleasure. It had occurred to Bonsoir—if he was to be absolutely honest, which he wouldn't have been—it had occurred to Bonsoir some days earlier that he could still remember the location of the treasure vault, hidden deep within the subterranean layers of the inner keep. And it had also occurred to Bonsoir that this vault, which under normal circumstances would have been so thickly guarded that even Bonsoir couldn't have had much hope of breaking into it, would, under these current conditions, likely be denuded of its normal compliment of soldiers. Worth looking into, at least. It was all well and good to enjoy your business, but Bonsoir was a professional, as has been mentioned, and a professional does not work for free.

There were some rats guarding the treasure chamber, though not nearly as many as usual. To get through them Bonsoir had to act with less subtlety than he preferred, tossing one of his few remaining sticks of dynamite, then coming in hard and fast with his knives in the second after it exploded. One of the rats got a shot off, but it went wide, and he didn't get a second. When the smoke cleared there were Bonsoir and three dead rats and a multicolored collage on the wall that Bonsoir assumed were the remains of a fourth.

It took nearly half an hour for Bonsoir to pick the lock, and he did not think he was being unduly arrogant—though Bonsoir was, admittedly, titanic in his self-regard—in saying that there was not another creature alive who could have managed it in twice the time. Still, it was longer than he liked to spend out in the open, with his back turned, and he felt his heart trill when the lock *snick*ed open, and he could slip inside.

Awaiting him was a clear blue spring to a creature dying of thirst; awaiting him were a mother's arms to a weeping babe; awaiting him was that final moment of release for which all living things secretly long. Even in these late days, after five years of misrule by Mephetic and five before that of civil war, the Gardens were a prosperous place, and the tax collectors ever busy. There were walls of scrip of all sorts, scrip from every one of the major banks and most of the kingdoms back east. But what is scrip, when compared with hard gold, heavy octagonal coins in thick cloth sacks, bars laid crossways? And what is gold compared to the innumerable glittering treasures, sterling jewelry and fat gemstones, emeralds and rubies and diamonds and things for which Bonsoir did not know the name?

It was the most beautiful sight that Bonsoir had ever seen, and he could not be blamed, or at least he could not have been blamed much, for the moment of shock that followed, for dropping his guard and staring in wonder at the wealth better than love that was now his.

But blame him or not, he paid for it.

"What a fascinating development," a voice said from behind him.

Bonsoir snarled and turned to throw one of his knives and felt something explode in the center of his torso. At first it was more a sensation of force than pain, but the pain came quickly on its heels, and the pain was worse than anything he had felt in a long life of misery. Then he was on the ground, and above him stood the handsomest little white cat you could ever want to see, grinning from ear to ear and watching Bonsoir bleed.

"By Cromwell's ghost," Puss said, "I hope they're not all in the bag so easy."

# Chapter 44

# Besting the Reaper

They were running through one of the many courtyards, heading toward the inner keep, Cinnabar in front, then the Captain, then Barley. They had given up being quiet but they were still trying to be quick, and so far they'd had no trouble, Cinnabar's hands making a handful of rats into a handful of corpses.

They had just passed the main guardhouse when the alarm bells began to ring. The Captain looked at Barley but didn't say anything. He didn't need to say anything; Barley had already unlimbered his cannon from off of his back, was checking on each of the little spinning bits and smiling brightly. The Captain continued on the way he was going, toward the heart of the castle. Cinnabar bothered with a good-bye, an uncharacteristic bit of sentimentality for the Dragon—and an unnecessary one.

Because Barley wasn't paying any attention; his eyes were huge and they were fixed on the guardhouse, and he wore a smile that was more of a leer, and after a quick moment, a very quick moment, Cinnabar followed the Captain, sprinting toward the inner keep. Barley gave the barrel of his gun one last spin, heard its familiar *clickety-clack*, and smiled wider. He began to walk backward slowly, till his great mass was blocking the path that the Captain had escaped down. He counted the seconds. He was as happy as a pup on Christmas morning, as a maid on her wedding night, as a wolf before his bloody red supper.

The first group of guards came out of the entrance, guns drawn and eyes wide with excitement, or perhaps terror. For certain it was terror in the next moment, the darkness of the courtyard lit by the muzzle-flash of the organ gun, a muzzle-flash that was blinding bright, a muzzle-flash that brought death with such speed and in such numbers that it seemed scarcely conceivable. Soon there was nothing left in the guardhouse—nothing left alive, I mean—and then and only then did Barley's gun go silent.

But it started up again a few minutes later, when reinforcements arrived, as loud as before and to the same effect. It took the rats a long time to realize they were better off not sprinting straight into the courtyard—rats are not known for their tactical sense. Really rats aren't known for much, except for being numerous and dying easily.

Or at least they died easily that day, even after they started taking cover in the surrounding buildings and trying to snipe at Barley. He was well positioned in the dark, and at this point the mounds of corpses he had made acted as cover. It took twenty minutes for one of the cleverer rodents to remember the heavy artillery, and another twenty to wheel one out from its position on the battlements. They wasted a lot of ammo finding the proper range, though they did a good job of destroying large sections of the castle.

And in the meantime Barley continued his work, *rat-tat-tat, rat-tat-tat.* And to find an equal to his tally, to do that bloody arithmetic—if one was inclined to do so, if one's mind ran in that sort of direction—one would have needed to compare him against disease, and time, and heartbreak.

Barley's body was never found. Of course, it wouldn't have been found even if it was there, not buried under all that rubble. Maybe, after the thing was over, after all of the killing was done, he shouldered up his cannon and disappeared again, this time making sure he buried himself so deep that no one, not even the Captain, could find him again. Or maybe the rats caught him with a shot from the howitzer, one of those shells goes off nearby and there's no need to worry about burial, not for a badger or a St. Bernard or a blue whale.

All that can be said with certainty is that when Barley did shuffle into the darkness, as all of us must, he had company waiting to meet him.

## Chapter 45

# Question Asked

Cinnabar was winding his way through the courtyard, the Captain in tow. The night echoed with Barley's covering fire, even a long way distant, drowning out the usual evening sounds. But all of a sudden, just the same, Cinnabar stopped, and the Captain stopped after him.

"What's going on?" the Captain asked, wise enough to know Cinnabar didn't do anything pointlessly.

"You go on ahead," Cinnabar said simply. "I've got business."

"You need any help?"

"No."

For a moment it seemed the Captain would say something. Cinnabar was his oldest friend, if the Captain could be said to have those. But perhaps he couldn't, because in the end he just scowled a little harder and hurried off.

When Brontë slipped from the shadows it was impossible to imagine she could have remained hidden for so long, given her size. But Brontë wasn't just big; Brontë was quick, and Brontë was agile, and if it hadn't been for Cinnabar's strangely keen perception Brontë might never have been noticed at all.

"I could have killed you both, just then," Brontë said, tapping the handle of the blunderbuss at her hip.

"You could have tried," Cinnabar said, rolling a cigarette.

Brontë was no stranger to the act itself, but never in her life had she seen it performed with such rapid precision, as if the salamander had willed the thing into existence. Maybe this made her nervous, and maybe that was why she started to talk.

"All the stories about you, I admit I'd expected more. The deadliest creature in the Gardens, the greatest gunslinger ever to slap iron. Mephetic still talks about you, about how many of his soldiers you killed. About some shoot-out near Black Fork where you put an entire family of rabbits into the ground in one go. And here you are, a mottled cold-blood in an old hat. But then I suppose that's the way of legends, to grow over-large in the telling."

Cinnabar sighed. How many times had he heard this line, how many dozens, maybe hundreds? Some mean-looking animal on the other end, trying to convince themselves that Cinnabar wasn't the most dangerous thing the gods had ever made. It had gotten so damn tiring, being the Dragon. If he had it to do again, Cinnabar sometimes thought, he wouldn't have become it.

Cinnabar lit his cigarette, took a long, slow drag on it, then let it fall to the ground and stamped it out with his heel. "I guess I should be easy killing, then."

Brontë's smile was mostly fang. "Deserved or not, you've got a big name. And when you die, I'll have a bigger one. Dragonslayer." Brontë let her palm stray down to her double-barreled cannon. "Dragonslayer. I like it."

Cinnabar didn't bother to respond, nor even to move his hands closer to his weapons. His eyes might have been taking in Brontë's movements, or they might have been staring at the moon that had risen, full and bright and beautiful, above the turrets of the inner keep.

Brontë went for her gun.

## Chapter 46

# Anticipation (3)

A half-mile out from the inner keep, hanging by her tail in the branches of a tall elm tree, unnoticeable in the darkness, Boudica adjusted her sights.

# Chapter 47

# Not a Frenchman

Bonsoir did not die neatly.

He was not a large creature, but he had a heart that belied his size, as does every trueborn son of Gaul. "You ought to take great pride, silly little kitten-creature," Bonsoir said. One hand pressed sharp against the hole in his stomach. The second pulled a crumpled cigarette from where it had rested behind his ear, set it in a mouth that was filling rapidly with blood, and lit it with a match. "For you have killed Bonsoir, the greatest assassin that Provence has ever produced."

Puss cocked his head, looked over at the several rats that had come into the treasure room after him, looked back at Bonsoir. "Excuse me?"

"I said you have killed Bonsoir, cousin of death; Bonsoir, who strikes in the night; Bonsoir, who—"

"What is that absurd accent?"

Bonsoir coughed up smoke, then blood. "If you had not put me down from behind, like the dastard you are,

Bonsoir would make you pay for the disrespect you show to his homeland."

"Your homeland, is it? *Et où êtes-vous, vous idiot peu hermine? Vous stupide, putois merde cerveau? Votre purulente, imbécile, faux chose?*"

Bonsoir didn't answer.

"No? Nothing? It's been so long since you've practiced your native tongue that you cannot even bother to recognize it?"

Still Bonsoir did not answer, though his eyes flashed with such hatred as one rarely sees apart from creatures who at one point loved one another.

"Are they such imbeciles in this country as not to have picked up on this mad deceit? How long have you been playing this absurd game? You're no more French than I am Sultan of Turkey!"

Puss laughed uproariously and turned to the rats that he had brought as backup, who laughed as well, less because they got the joke and more because you laugh if the creature above you laughs—at least you do if you are a rat, who are creatures not unpracticed in obsequiousness. Puss giggled and guffawed, Puss chuckled and chortled, Puss cackled and tittered and howled, Puss all but ruptured his diaphragm in amusement.

It was a very loud laugh. It was not, however, the last one.

# Chapter 48

# Question Answered

Perhaps, somewhere in the world, since the dawn of history, there was someone as fast as Cinnabar. The Gardens are vast, and time is long. Regardless, Brontë was not that creature. Before she had unholstered her weapon Cinnabar had released an entire chamber from the revolver on his right hip, fanning a cluster of shots that curdled the cream of the fox's eye a cherry red. Brontë screamed and let off a shot that flew well to the left of the salamander, who by this point had dropped his empty revolver and repeated the trick with its full twin, sending another round of metal into the neck and scalp of the fox.

Brontë would never be as fast as Cinnabar, nowhere near, but she was a damn sight bigger. The dozen pricks of lead the Dragon had set into her flesh were insufficient to put her down, indeed barely enough to slow her. As the salamander dropped his empty weapon and moved to draw the one from his boot Brontë fired the second barrel on her blunderbuss.

Nothing is faster than a bullet, but Cinnabar was close. As Brontë's hand cannon erupted Cinnabar dropped low to the ground and launched himself sideways. If the fox's weapon fired solid shot he might even have made it, but as it was the outer edge of the cloud of shrapnel ripped into Cinnabar's side, leaving bits of entrails peeking through his skin.

Her ammunition depleted, Brontë dove at Cinnabar, anxious to finish with claws and teeth what she had started with her pearl-handled shotgun. Off-balance from his wounds, the salamander still managed to dance aside, sending another wave of fire into her torso.

To little enough avail. Every shot Cinnabar had fired found purchase in the more sensitive portions of Brontë's flesh, but each injury seemed only to enrage her further. She turned back around on the salamander, hissed madly, and charged a second time.

This time Cinnabar didn't try to dodge. With an agility that belied the leaking corner of his intestine he unlimbered the half-rifle and steadied it at the coming behemoth. Cinnabar's hands worked the lever, sent a flurry of lead into his enemy. Tufts of pink brain and white bone and red fur flew out of Brontë's skull, but it did nothing to slow her momentum. She barreled forward with sufficient force to topple the Dragon, already unsteady from his wounds. They tumbled together,

Brontë dead but not knowing it, Cinnabar dying and certain of the fact.

When it was done Cinnabar lay pinned beneath the aerated corpse of the fox, now finally still. Cinnabar's hat, which had been knocked off in the struggle, was a few inches out of his reach. He strained with every fiber of the part of his body that still worked, grabbed the Stetson, and set it over his forehead.

Then he sighed, and stared up at the moon, and breathed once more, and allowed himself to die.

## Chapter 49

# Reunion

The Captain hurried toward the inner keep, sprinting along the high edge of the ramparts, alone so far as could be seen. Barley's cannon went silent, finally, and the night returned to its stillness. And then that stillness—which was a false stillness, a stillness that is the preface to noise—was filled with a low shuddering, the sound of an unclean death.

Some creatures say that the rattlesnake is misunderstood, that he makes his telltale sound to warn of his danger and ward off misfortune for all parties. Some creatures are fools. No snake can be trusted, and the rattler least of all. He does not rattle to alert—he rattles to threaten, he rattles to mock. He rattles to let you know that he can bring you death, if he so chooses, and that doing so would be a joy for him, indeed would be his chief joy.

The sound got louder and louder, and then it was joined by scale slithering along stone, and finally by the sight of the snake's flesh, pale as an exsanguinated corpse.

"Captain," the Quaker said, the last word elongated over his forked tongue. "How long it's been, and how much I have missed you, you and all my old companions."

When last the Captain had seen the Quaker he had been young and bright green and filled three-deep with creatures he had swallowed during that last horrible evening, creatures who had thought themselves friends to the beast, who were foolish enough to imagine that a serpent has a heart in any but the most literal sense.

The Captain didn't move, his hands in the pockets of his duster, a scowl on his face. "Did you now? All of us?"

"Alas for Gertrude, amiable as fair death! I take it that was Barley making so much noise earlier. But there is no noise any longer, is there, and I suppose we can guess what that means. Bonsoir always preferred silence; one way or the other I won't be seeing him. And I know that Brontë had a special surprise prepared for Cinnabar, though I doubt things will work out quite the way the fox planned."

"And?"

"Boudica? But she won't be anywhere nearby."

"And?" the Captain asked. "And? And?"

Quaker looked at the Captain a long while. Then he looked all about himself, into the deep dark stillness of the night. Then he smiled.

Elf shot from one of the crevices that the evening reserves for itself, shrieking her shriek that was the last thing so many creatures had heard, squirrels and mice and rats and bats and polecats and skunks. Where had she been? Not so small a bird, if not so large either, and she couldn't fly anymore, hobbled by the *click-click-click* of her talons. But that night she had moved as stealthily as Bonsoir, or a shadow, which was to say the same thing.

They moved with a speed that was impossible to follow, feinting and striking, each attack shading imperceptibly into the next such that determining individual movements was impossible. The Quaker snapped and twisted, hoping to wrap himself around his old lover in one final, deadly embrace. Elf avoided this kindness, offering her own with a beak that shone bright in the moonlight, and talons that she'd kept sharp as her hate. She should have been easy prey for the snake, old and mottled and flightless as she was. But this proved not to be the case, for after a full forty-five seconds—which is an eternity in mortal combat, which is longer than perhaps any other creature in the Gardens would have lasted with either—the contest remained undecided.

Furious at this difficulty, the Quaker turned smoothly from Elf and launched himself at the Captain, as swiftly as a ball from a cannon, with no doubt the same effect had he reached the mouse. But in the instant before he would have struck, Elf intercepted the Quaker's movement with one of her own, just as potent and fierce; with a flap of her wings she cast herself forward into the rattler, claws finding the soft tissue around his eyes. The Quaker did not scream: not when the blood began to come swiftly down his face, not when the force of Elf's attack carried both of them tumbling out over the walls and down into the ether, the desperate and hoped-for outcome, a fatal embrace descending, together forever, into the darkness.

# Chapter 50

# Good Night

"Imagine," Puss continued, gesturing widely to his soldiers. "Years affecting this mad conceit, and no one ever bothered to call him on it! What strange, pathetic creatures you breed on this side of the pond! This sad little ermine has spent the entirety of his life pretending to be something he is not, as if massacring his vowels offered some patina of class. What is that sound?"

What *was* that sound? It was something like sand leaking through an hourglass, or silk running across a lady's hand. It wasn't either of these things, of course, though it had more in common with the first.

What it was, in fact, as Puss realized after he had turned around, was the thin little string attached to the end of Bonsoir's last stick of dynamite rapidly being eaten away by flame.

"I am not an ermine!" Bonsoir said, blood bubbling up past his smile.

Puss's eyes went very wide. He prepared to do something, though what that something would have been never did become clear.

Puss was cultured, Puss was clever, Puss was fast and cruel and deadly—but Puss was not wise. For, if Bonsoir was no Frenchman, he was, most certainly, a stoat. And if a Frenchman is many things, at the end of the day, a stoat is only one—a killer.

And now the fuse was a fingernail, and now a hair's breadth.

"Bonsoir!" Bonsoir said.

# Chapter 51

# One Final Ace

The Captain entered the inner keep as alone in reality as he had always been in spirit. He skirted from shadow to shadow, eyes wary, one hand on the shotgun strapped to his back—but there arrived no excuse for using it, and he passed into the throne room without incident.

It had been used to crown the Lords and Ladies of the Gardens for untold generations, it was gold and silver; it was cool stone and buffed ivory; it was soft samite and thick Oriental silk. From the stained-glass windows above, the Toads' forebears observed the proceedings with regal disinterest. The throne was large enough to have accommodated a wolfhound, and Mephetic, lounging on the lip, seemed lost amid its grandeur. He had one hand on a box detonator, a coil of string leading off into the darkness. He had the other around a bottle of brown liquor.

"You might not believe this, but I'm about to do you a favor."

"Yeah?"

"Absolutely. Being in charge of the Gardens is not all it's cracked up to be. Monetary policy, tax revenue, the bureaucracy . . . Trust me, it's mostly hassle. Taking it was the only part I really liked."

"Where's the Younger?"

"Struggling with an opium suppository, if I had to guess. The Lord is not one to let a little thing like revolution get in the way of pleasure. Anyway, who cares? He was never the point of the thing."

"No," the Captain agreed. "Just want to make sure it all gets wrapped up."

"I've rigged enough dynamite to send the entire inner keep to the moon," Mephetic said, laughing. "Don't worry. We'll be taking the Lord with us." Mephetic took a long, slow slug of whiskey, making sure to keep an eye on the Captain while he did so. When he was done, he put the top on the bottle and tossed it to the mouse. "One last nip before we meet the devil?"

The Captain caught it with one hand, uncorked it, and took a swig. The other hand he raised above his head.

# Chapter 52

# Resolution

A half-mile out from the inner keep, hanging by her tail in the branches of a tall elm tree, unnoticeable in the darkness, Boudica fired.

# Chapter 53

# The Builders

There was the sound of a window breaking, and then Mephetic's head disappeared.

Not disappeared, so much as redistributed itself, on the ground and the wall and the throne itself. The Captain waved again, unnecessarily. Boudica had seen well enough to make the shot; of course she could see well enough to know she hadn't missed. Not that Boudica ever missed.

The Captain drank what was left in the bottle with one protracted gulp. Then he let it shatter against the floor and moved on, swiftly but not hurrying, into the hallway that lay beyond the throne room.

The corridor stank terribly, and it stank worse the farther he went, and the Captain knew he was close. At the end of the passageway was a door, and beyond that door was a room, and inside that room was evidence that no creature should have all its desires fulfilled. The chamber was as foul as any abattoir, cut-rate whorehouse, or public toilet. The Captain had not seen the creature that breathed at the center of it for ten years, since before the start of the War of the Two Brothers, and in the interim he had gotten fatter and nastier but not fundamentally different in any other way.

The Lord was larger than any toad you'd ever expect to see, nearly as big as Barley was, or had been, or whatever. Though of course the badger's size had been mostly muscle, whereas the Lord was so grotesquely obese that he couldn't walk unaided, could only lift his arms with difficulty. The collection of warts, humps, swollen bulges, and goiters would have done credit to a colony of lepers. His eyes were as dim as a miner's candle, and it took him a long time to react to this new development.

"You," the Lord said. Somewhere in the dim recesses of his amphibious brain, a brain that had long been subject to the degrading effects of every vice and narcotic that had ever been invented or distilled, a connection was made. "I remember you. You were . . . you were my brother's, weren't you?"

"He was mine, would be a better way of putting it."

The Lord looked at the Captain slyly for a moment, and asked, "Are you real?"

"Real as anything."

"Then those sounds I was hearing, all that gunfire and screaming—that was real too? Not just inside my mind?"

The Captain nodded.

The Lord took a few long seconds to work through the arithmetic. "Then that means you're here to kill me."

"You weren't first on the list," the Captain informed him. "But you are the last one left."

The Lord did not say anything for a long time. He was working very hard to piece the puzzle together, though it was no easy thing for a creature who had been required to do nothing more difficult than light his hash pipe for the better part of a decade.

But he managed it, and in doing so he received a sudden and unexpected burst of energy, one that propelled him into monologue. "Well? Where is he? Where is my elder brother, who has so long been absent from my bosom? Let me show him all the deference due one whose birth was a full five minutes before my own." The toad's face, unlovely under the best of circumstances, was further marred with the molasses-thick swell of fraternal hatred. It had been so long since the toad had been required to perform any physical act more tiring than evacuating waste or receiving pleasure that even this short oration left him exhausted and out of breath, his warty hide rising and falling, rising and falling.

The Captain didn't say anything for a while, just watched the Lord try to breathe. He was carrying a small burden on his back, and he removed it and rolled it out onto the floor.

The Lord's eyes throbbed out from his skull. His mouth hung open; his tongue uncoiled itself until it nearly touched the fat of his belly.

Laid against the bed of the now-unraveled satchel was a collection of bones picked clean by time. Amid these remnants was a jet-white skull, a skull that was unquestionably that of a toad.

"I know he was alive when he reached the Kingdom to the South," the Captain said. "So he must have died some time afterward. It might have been natural. Or it might not have been. I suppose down there they figured he kept his value as a potential threat, so long as Mephetic never found out."

"But . . . then . . ." The Lord's great bulbous jaw jiggled inanely. "What was the point?"

The last Lord of the Gardens died miserably and without fanfare, the Captain offering both barrels, shrapnel spreading putrescent green rot against the wall. The toad was so corpulent that at first it seemed the loss of a half his body weight wouldn't be enough to kill him, and the Captain started to reload his weapon. But then the Lord let out a loud, wet fart, near as foul as Mephetic's stink, and he slunk down into his chair.

When the Captain got back to the throne room he found an ancient vole in faded livery, looking out the window at the ruined keep below, and the city beyond it which would soon see nothing but chaos, and the country past that which would know the same. "So much death," he said. "So much death."

The Captain stopped in front of him and shrugged, as if he had seen more.

"What happens now?" the servant asked, too old to be frightened. "The keep is in ruins, the country devastated. All this slaughter, and what will come of it? Who will rule the Gardens now? Who will rebuild?"

The Captain pulled out a cigar from beneath his coat. The Captain cut the tip off. The Captain put it to his mouth. The Captain lit the end. The Captain breathed in deep, and exhaled a river of smoke.

"We don't build."

# Acknowledgments

*The Builders* has a special place in my heart, being essentially a one-note joke that remains funny for me five-odd years after I came up with it—thanks to you, the reader, for indulging my adolescent sensibilities! Professional thanks to Justin Landon, Lee Harris, Jared Shurin, and Chris Kepner. Aesthetic appreciation to my obvious stylistic influences, including but not limited to Frederick Forsyth, Akira Kurosawa, Sergio Leone, Sam Peckinpah, and William Goldman. Thanks to family and friends; for the roll call you can look at every other book I published and strike off the ex-girlfriends.

# About the Author

DANIEL POLANSKY was born in Baltimore in 1984. He was living in Brooklyn when he wrote this, but by the time you read it he might be somewhere else.

# TOR·COM

**Science fiction. Fantasy.**
**The universe.**
**And related subjects.**

*

More than just a publisher's website, Tor.com
is a venue for **original fiction, comics,** and
**discussion** of the entire field of SF and fantasy,
in all media and from all sources. Visit our site
today—and join the conversation yourself.

CPSIA information can be obtained at www.ICGtesting.com
Printed in the USA
LVOW07s1939301015

460471LV00004B/147/P